MEMORIES
AND OTHER FICTIONS

Novels by Richard S. Platz

OF MAGIC AND DELUSION

PROJECT DIVINE WIND

APPOINTMENT AT ANGAHUAN
(Co-Authored with James A. Kline)

MEMORIES
AND OTHER FICTIONS
Short Stories of Richard S. Platz

Blue Lake Press

BLUE LAKE PRESS
A Western Division Subsidiary of the
Chicago, Whitewater & Mad River Company
P O Box 797, Blue Lake, CA 95525

ISBN: 978-0692202746

Contents

Preface

The eyes of a strange old man stare into mine in wonder. Or is it dread? They are tired eyes. Inquisitive eyes. Guileless eyes. Skin sags around the corners. Around the nose. The jowls. The neck is wattled. The hair has grown as white and thin as spider silk. A disappointed scowl twists the thin lips downward in a stern verdict.

It is my father's scowl.

I wipe the condensate from the mirror to see more clearly. *What does this old man want of me?* He mimics me as my fingers trace the surgical scar in the center of my chest, as if exploring a surface more easily penetrated. To what lies beneath the image. Behind the mask. *Inside.*

I have grown old. That I cannot deny. But, madly, *inside* I am still young. I still *remember*. All of it, by god! The foolish lyrics of rock-and-roll songs of half a century ago. The bursting ache and dizziness of high school desire. The crushing depression of rejection and defeat. The folly of two failed marriages. The real. The imagined. *All of it I remember!*

So clear it all seems. The veil of concealment is gone with the fog from the mirror. I see that so much of what once consumed me—so vital, so crucial, so *dangerous*—was no more than a soap opera. A thunderous play poorly written and badly acted, rich in color and patina like an old coffee can rusting by the backyard fence, but of no more consequence.

But I do not trust this clarity. The story of my life, that internal narrative which preoccupies my mind and is inseparable from my thoughts, is a fiction. In this bathroom mirror I see what I have become. I am disappointed, of course. Disappointed that the worst has come to pass. But I no longer find it frightful. Loathsome, perhaps. Disappointing, yes. But nothing any longer to fear.

Who am I to judge this man who faces me? This wrinkled residue of so many dreams and desires and disappointments who drips before me in the fog-rimmed glass. This face of an ordinary life. I would like to say, "I have done my best," but I know that would be untrue. I know I could have done better. All along, I could have done better. Now it is too late. The wine has spilled from the bottle. Death concentrates itself in the dregs, permeating what little time is left.

But no matter! This reflection and I have been dying our entire lives, day by day, and there are so few days left to fuss over that I have to smile. *He* smiles. In the mirror, he smiles as if we have finally found common ground. A pleasant little joke to share between us. We who have always been so at odds.

I whip the mug soap into a thick froth and paint the lather across my cheeks, dab it under my nose and beneath my chin. That strange old man in the mirror does the same, mimicking every move. Mocking me. But his smug taunt does not intimidate me. I know it to be false. An empty facade. Beneath the stern demeanor the old man lives in fear. Like my father, deep inside he is afraid.

The razor scrapes my flesh. I have always been afraid. For as long as I can remember. Afraid of what is. Afraid of what might come to be. Afraid of what *I* might become. Of what I might do. Of failure. Of ridicule. Fear is woven into the helical coil of my destiny. As inherent as the color of my eyes. But fear is losing its grip. It is evaporating, mingling into the background echo of absurdity. As the remaining years dwindle to an eviscerated few, it becomes hard to imagine myself more ridiculous than I have already become.

One of my earliest memories is as a child, lying in the grass and clover and watching a puffy white cloud float across the azure sky. The breeze carries the drone of a summer airplane. I can not actually *see* the cloud move, and this makes me impatient, as all children are impatient. I look away for as long as I can endure, and when I gaze back, I measure how much progress that lazy cloud had made in its drift to the other side of a nearby branch.

Now, at the opposite end of a life filled with the tricks that time can play, I am no longer so impatient. I believe that now I can actually see the movement of the clouds. Soon I will be able to watch the grass grow. The world speeds up as I slow down. I will one day be as motionless as the stones, and then the world will wheel past dizzyingly until the end of time.

And then these roiling memories will have ceased to be internal. They will become mere scars and scratches on the surface of an uninhabited planet. I immerse my face in the warm, soapy water and a sea of recollections. Rivulets run down my cheeks and chin, as they do from his in the mirror. Those fevered eyes implore me to pick a handful of blossoms from these vast fields of golden poppies, stretching beyond the horizon in every direction, and to make a bouquet of our most special memories to preserve in a timeless crystal vase of words.

Here then is a handful of short stories, composed from my memories and from my imagination. They are recollections and they are fictions. That is to say, they are all fictions.

April 2014
Blue Lake, California

Prayer

I stand outside myself, watching myself watching myself.
I smile, I smile, I smile.
  – from *The Ruling Class* by Peter Barnes

1

I jerked alert as a small white sign blurred past in the headlights. "Pull over there," I coughed, pointing through the bug-spattered windshield to a swath of wide shoulder glowing ahead like a nebula in the darkness.

"Where?" the driver asked, easing his foot off the gas.

"Over there," I repeated. "This's Dutchtown. This's where I get off."

The pickup veered off the blacktop, fishtailed into a broad gravel parking area illuminated by a single street light, and crunched to a dusty stop. Beside us loomed a dimly-lit corrugated metal building with a couple of gas pumps out front. The lights were all off, but I could just make out "Swamp Garage" in faded letters, blistering and black, above the doors. A sandwich board advertised regular gasoline for 26.9 cents.

In the ghostly glow of the dashboard lights, the brown-skinned driver looked concerned. "You' sure gonna have a hell of a time catching another ride from here," he said. "Don't even look like a town to me."

"Yeah," I agreed, cracking open the door and unfolding my stiff body slowly onto the gravel. "Sure doesn't look like much." I reached for my duffle bag behind the seat. "But once I get on the road, anyone coming by will probably give me a lift. They're pretty friendly around here."

"T' white folks, maybe," he grinned. "An that's' *if* anybody comes by. Where'd you say you was goin' again?"

"A little town called Whitewater. It's really not that far, as I recall.

Just a couple of miles. My grandmother has a house there."

"Well, she's sure gonna be surprised t'be woke up in the middle a'the night."

"Won't even have to wake her up," I said. I didn't tell him that she wouldn't be there. That she was lying semiconscious in a nursing home hundreds of miles away in Illinois. That I intended to break into the empty house. I held out my hand. "But I gotta thank you for the ride. If you hadn't'a picked me up, I'd probably still be standing on a street corner in Cape Girardeau with my thumb stuck out."

"Oh, 's'nothin'." He shook my hand. "Glad t'help y'out. But you sure I can't drop ya someplace with a little more traffic?"

"Wouldn't be goin' my way. I can walk this if I have to. But thanks anyhow." I slammed the door and watched him pull back out on the long, empty two-lane of US 25. His tail lights shrank into a single red spot, then disappeared, bound heaven knows where in the flat farmlands of southeastern Missouri.

The driver's comments made me think of something my grandmother had once told me years ago. I had asked her whether they had any problems with Negroes there in Whitewater. "No," she had been quick to reply. "Not at all. Not since we drove'em all out'a town t' Allenville."

I gazed around. A few lights burned in the distance, beyond the corona of the street lamp. A porch lantern. A light on a high pole. A few windows glowed dimly from invisible farm houses imbedded in the surrounding plain of blackness. There was no sound of traffic on the highway. Frogs croaked from the drainage ditches. A lonely dog howled somewhere to the west, and another barked an answer nearby. A quarter moon hung half-way down the western sky. The night was already growing chilly, blunting the fecund agricultural ripeness of the November air, so I zipped up my jacket, picked up my duffle, and started walking south, the same direction my last ride had gone.

The road map showed all the routes converging on Dutchtown, but no detail on how they met. I was looking for State Highway A, heading west toward Whitewater. Since I hadn't seen a sign for the turnoff from the truck, I figured it was still a little ways up the highway. In a quarter-mile I found a white wooden marker beneath another lonely street lamp. It pointed right and read, "Whitewater 9 mi." Nine miles! That was farther than I had figured. How long was it going to take to hoof it nine miles? Two hours. Three? More?

Never mind. I was in pretty decent shape. I could walk nine miles if I had to. And maybe a ride would come along. I didn't have a whole lot of options. I wondered what time it had gotten to be. In answer, the lights in the windows of a distant farm house winked off, one by one. What time do farmers go to bed? It was probably ten o'clock already. Maybe later. And I was just starting out.

I shifted the weight of my duffle to my left hand and started west down the empty road. The street lights and farmhouses of Dutchtown slowly receded and disappeared behind me, but the low quarter moon offered plenty of luminance to find my way along the pearly white gravel of the deserted road. The fields on either side were vast seas of darkness, punctuated here and there with remote islands of light from far distant farms. The night pulsed with the chorus of crickets and frogs. As I fell into a rhythm, occasionally shifting my bag from arm to arm, warm inside my thin cotton jacket, I had plenty of time to think about how I had gotten into this pickle.

Kerouac and Bethany came to mind. Bethany and Kerouac. They seemed to me to be the twin blades of a scissors cutting the fabric of my destiny. Kerouac because he wrote a book. And Bethany . . . *oh, Bethany!*

I had consumed Jack Kerouac's novel *On the Road* as if it had been written just for me. It chronicled and glorified the antics of an irresponsible buffoon named Dean Moriarity as he hitchhiked around the country. Moriarity was a thinly disguised avatar of Neal Cassidy, a self-indulgent show-off who I never would have taken to if ever I had met him face to face. But Moriarity the character was a breath of fresh air, an iconoclast in a world dearly needing one. And Kerouac was the voice of the Beat Generation.

You have to remember that this was back in the sunset of the Eisenhower years. The halcyon days when my family would watch *Ozzie and Harriet* together and concur that nothing in the universe was out of order. Nothing irrational would ever happen. But I knew in my bones that something was fundamentally wrong. Something was out of joint. Mostly I thought it was just me. I didn't fit in. I was still a scrawny high school kid looking for a way out. No longer a child. Not yet a man. And through a threadbare seam in the illusion, I rooted for Elvis as he offended the established, and for James Dean as he rebelled against the hypocritical. I longed to be a writer like Kerouac. So I took to hitchhiking.

Over that Thanksgiving week vacation I hitchhiked to Missouri. Without telling anyone, I packed my duffle bag and stuck out my thumb heading south from northern Illinois. No one knew where I was going. Or, for a while, that I was even gone. I can't remember many of the people who picked me up and dropped me off. I do remember a long, dispiriting wait for a ride near the Caterpillar plant outside Springfield, when I almost gave up and skulked back home. But a big-rig trucker finally gave me a ride in his cab-over, all the way to the outskirts of Saint Louis, and the die was cast. There would be no turning back.

The house in Whitewater had been my destination all along. I had memories of the place from family visits when my Grandmother still lived there. My fascination as a child made the place a magnet. The oddity of no indoor plumbing. An outhouse instead, down a secret path through the tall corn. The squeaking of the hand pump crank as it raised water from the cistern below ground. The slam of the screen doors. Forbidden freedom to pee outside on the green grass before bedtime. The strange husks of cicada shells, like invading aliens, lifelessly gripping the coarse bark of the surrounding shade trees. The pop of firecrackers and the fiery balls of the roman candles in July. The creak of the porch swing in the sultry summer afternoon. The oily smell of insecticide hand-pumped from a spray can. Coal smoke, thunder, and the terrible whistle of the afternoon steam locomotive. I wanted to see if any of it still remained.

But things had not turned out as I had imagined. Delays had put me on this gravel road well into the night. As the moon sank into a bank of clouds on the western horizon, the hedgerows lining the road became black shapes eclipsing the stars. I was afraid. Of course I was. The landscape I traversed was a foreign, fearful place, made more so by its invisibility. A low, constant dread vibrated from the pale road and the dark, indecipherable fields. I was beyond everything familiar. Perhaps beyond the rational. This uneasiness erupted in the bark of a dog, disturbed by the crunch of my footsteps, and echoed far and away in the rippling howls of animals spreading across the alien farmland. Darkness manifested my fear, became the membrane through which I inexorably pushed. I felt it. I accepted it. I tried to dial it down. Keep it on leash. Until another dog suddenly growled beside the road, unseen through some dark shrubbery that may or may not have contained a fence, jolting my heart with a fresh pulse of adrenalin.

As my quickened strides carried me farther into the fields, away from all outposts of civilization, the fear subsided into the background chirping and croaking and became the dull pounding of a distant surf. But in the vacuum it left, a familiar ache arose to replace it. My lips formed the word, *"Bethany."*

Bethany was her name. Bethany Jean Harwood. As I write this, that name no longer shivers me with any magic at all. Her face has long since sunk into the fog bank of time. But on that lonely, black, cold night, my boots crunching along the interminable gravel, the sound of her name and the vision of her face and the remembrance of her breasts and slender young shoulders weakened my knees. My heart swelled to aching. Physical aching. My breathe came shallow and quick.

For Bethany was the first love of my life. And, I believed then, she would be my last. For how could I survive without her? I had been sixteen when one rapturous evening, with the first snow falling lightly outside the windows of her parent's cozy living room, she had stolen my heart with kisses and caresses and the unspoken promise of love. Enthralled, I had given her my heart, and she had devoured it in a single bite. But in the sobering days that followed, Bethany changed. She kept her distance and turned to look upon me with indifference. Pity even. Oh! hate and loathing would have been a kinder fate. Her indifference was unbearable.

Bethany, I should add, was a devout Christian. The first, but not the last devout Christian I would fall foolishly in love with. I could never figure out why I have been such a sucker for Christian women. Perhaps it was that cloak of vulnerability, all frilled and fluffed and fancied over a hard-rock core of irrational certitude. An insane cocksureness in the face of the obvious hopelessness, chaos, and death. But all that is another story for another time.

After the moon had set completely, the Milky Way blazed its bright swath of stars from horizon to horizon. Orion hovered overhead, creeping westward, forever chasing the Pleiades. Oh, how well I knew that vane pursuit. I trudged on by starlight, the white gravel roadway glowing faintly in a landscape of blackness. The night grew steadily colder. Cold enough to stiffen the fingers of the hand clutching my duffle bag, so that I had to switch them frequently and plunge the free hand into the warmth of my jacket pocket. My nose began to run a little. But my body stayed warm from the exertion. A damp perspiration ringed my neck beneath my turned-up collar.

I had nothing but time as the night wore on. Time to muse. Time to consider the bigger questions. Was God up there watching me, I wondered. Behind the stars as I trudged through the valley of the shadow of death? Was He *with* me? I could never quite visualize God. The concept of the Holy Trinity left me cold. It seemed a wives' tale invented for children. But God *Himself*. What was *He*? I had some vague notion of a vast Being overseeing the workings of the universe, considering every detail of my life and everyone else's. An emotional Palpability I could not define. A Heavenly Father, whatever that might mean. But was God really up there? Was He aware of me at that moment. Aware of my long walk. Aware of how I suffered?

It occurred to me that I should pray. It was not so much a compulsion as a logical conclusion. Right there on that gravel road beneath the gleaming stars. Part of me was willing to try just about anything. Another part was embarrassed by the ridiculous notion. And yet a third part said, "Hey, why not? No one is ever going to know."

So I set down my bag and tried to remember just how to go about it. Years had passed since I had last prayed. Prayed as a child prays. But my hands came together easily in the mudra of prayer. I knelt upon the rocky ballast of that less-traveled road. But my mind remained as divided as the cold stars above. As I knelt, I watched myself bend, and I watched myself kneel, and I knew that it would all be futile. Misguided. Absurd. But I bore down and by sheer will pressed on. Deep inside some core of blind faith oozed up to seek the cleansing supplication of prayer. It longed to be washed in the blood of the Lamb. Wanted to leave nothing undone, even as my mind saw this exercise as nothing more than the gaudy dumbshow of a clown. Faith and mockery were intertwined within the helix of my life.

I waited for it to come, then out loud I spoke the only words that seemed to matter. "God, please make Bethany love me. Soften her heart and bring her back to me." I waited for more, but nothing more came. "If you do," I added, as a sort of quid pro quo to seal the deal, "I will try to be the best person I can be." I hoped that was enough. "Amen."

For a while I went on kneeling, as an improbable saint might go on kneeling, trying to close out the things of this world, awaiting a sign of God's presence. Waiting for something to happen. I waited until my hands and feet grew numb and the cold seeped in through my collar. I began to shiver. Stiffly I stood, blew into my cupped fingers, then hoisted my bag and resumed walking.

2

The road seemed it would never end. Not a single car came by. My shoulders ached from the relentless tug and swing of the duffle bag, which grew heavier with each mile. My fatigue edged towards exhaustion. There was no end in sight. I could not stop for even a short rest, lest the damp cold of my sweaty t-shirt might bring back cold shivers. My thoughts grew incoherent. Dreamlike. Again and again I tried to estimate when I had reached the half-way point, then the three-quarters mark, and I watched for the glow of lights of Whitewater. But the unending stretch of pale, cold road ahead defied my calculations. It *couldn't* be much farther, I thought. But it was. And the night wore on like a bad dream.

More than once I thought I was trudging through a small community, but it was probably just a sleeping farmhouse near the road. Dogs barked fiercely from close by. Long after I stopped trying to figure where I was, I came to a major fork in the road. It was a wye. I could find no road sign, and it was too dark to read my map. The main tracks seemed to continue left, but it was hard to decipher them in the starlit gravel. I kept to the left and hoped I was still on route.

My mind grew as numb as my fingers. My shoulders and back ached. Mechanically I trudged onward. Then at last, far ahead, I saw the dim glow of lights. Perhaps a mile further the road climbed a small hill with a cross-street and dark houses on each side. As I crested the hill, more structures appeared below in the glare of a half-dozen street lamps at intersecting gravel streets. Two blocks ahead stood the white wooden railroad crossing sign. I had made it!

I recognized Whitewater at once in the glare of the few scattered street lamps. I crossed Church Street, then dropped down to Main Street, which was separated from the railroad tracks by a strip of untended weeds. I turned left, walked a block, and there it was, on the far corner beyond the house where our playmate Louis Frances had grown up. Lit by a street lamp behind me and one across the tracks, my grandmother's two-story frame farmhouse rose ghostly white and proud among the black branches of sturdy old shade trees. It stood at the front of a large lot that stretched up to the next block where the church presided. I remembered those shade trees. I remembered the house. The windows were dark. In fact, no one seemed to be awake in the whole damned town.

I pushed open the low gate and followed the crumbling sidewalk up to the big, open front porch. Two wooden swings hung by chains from the boarded ceiling, just as I remembered. I dumped my duffle onto one of the swings and tried the front door. It was locked. A single mortised lock below a curtained window secured the door. No deadbolt. No padlock. I examined the key hole and concluded that any skeleton key could probably open it. But I had no skeleton key.

I walked around to the back, pulled open the screen door, and stepped into the big screened porch. The back door to the kitchen was locked too. Slowly I circled the house, testing the ground floor windows all the way around. They were all closed and locked. Returning to the front, I began to shiver. It was cold, and I was exhausted. *What was I going to do?*

Blowing into my hands and rubbing them together, I gazed up at the second-story windows of the sleeping room above the front porch. Perhaps one of them was unlocked. But how to get up there? Maybe if I stood on one of the banisters behind a swing, I could pull myself up to try one. Pushing past the swing on the left, the one that was best lit by the street lights, I climbed up and balanced on the white railing, steadying myself with the round corner post. I could not reach the windows, but found that I could get a finger-hold on the ledge just below them. With numb fingers I stretched and grasped and swung myself out over the dark shrubs beside the porch. A slow chin-up brought my face up to the level of my hands, then bracing myself with my right hand and my ankles clamped around the corner post, I reached with my left and pushed up on the bottom edge of the nearest window. *It rose a little!*

I rebraced my legs and pushed up harder. The window slid open about eight inches, as far as I could reach. I was now able to grasp the sill, but my hands were growing weary. By twisting my elbows outward and letting go with my legs, I managed to swing my other hand onto the sill too. For a moment I just dangled there, catching my breath. One more chin-up is all it was going to take, but my arms had grown weak as the blood drained out of them. I strained, but couldn't pull myself up. I just couldn't do it. I hung there exhausted, gazing down at the shrubbery fifteen feet below me. I was stuck.

My hands were in danger of losing their grip, so I began to swing my legs back and forth like a pendulum to provide a little extra oomph for the chin-up. On a big back swing I strained my arms, I wriggled, I kicked my feet, and slowly I pulled myself up far enough to get my right arm inside the window, after nudging it open further with the top of my head. I managed to drag myself upward and through, scraping my arms and my chest painfully over the sill, and tumbled headfirst into the warmth of the upstairs room.

A second story man, I grinned to myself as I lay there panting. I sat up and looked out the window to see if anyone was watching. I wondered if anyone had called the sheriff to report a break in. But the town appeared to sleep. All was still. I pulled the window shut and stood up.

Light from the street lamp lit a surface-mounted wall switch beside the door. I tried it, but no light came on. I felt for another at the top of the steep, dark stairwell, flicked it up, with the same result. The power had apparently been turned off. So I fumbled my way down into the blackness of those steep stairs by clinging to the banister like a fire pole and feeling the risers with my toes. I found my way into the kitchen, where the distant street light shone through the windows and gleamed off a kerosene lamp on the table. I found a box of wooden matches on the window ledge next to a wash bowl and porcelain pitcher, struck one, lit the lamp, then trimmed back the wick so it wouldn't smoke. The room was bathed in a soft yellow glow.

I gazed around the kitchen. The wood-burning, cast-iron Wedgewood I remembered so well was gone, replaced by a plain white electric range. Without power, that would do me no good. Nor would the refrigerator on the opposite wall, its door propped open by a straw broom. The familiar, long forgotten aroma of wood smoke and ripe crops and old things long stored in an attic, an ambiance impossible to describe, wafted back visions and intimations from my earliest times there. Recollections from childhood. From long before Kerouac. Long before Bethany. Before the onslaught of adolescence. From before the world had grown complicated. I breathed it all in as a kind of relaxation therapy. A deep breath of perspective. I had made it here, and in that regard, all was well.

On the counter I found an old red plastic flashlight that still worked, which I carried with me to look around the first floor of the old house. Keys sprouted from the inside of the locks on both the front and kitchen doors. I opened the front door and retrieved my duffle bag. I stepped out the back door and peed in the damp grass. I cranked the handle of the rotary pump on the concrete slab outside the back door, and the clank-clank-clanking, which seemed too loud for the middle of the night, radiated across the sleeping town. A surge of water spilled out of the spout, so I retrieved the pitcher from inside and managed to raise enough water to fill it. Greedily I drank my fill.

I carried the kerosene lamp into my grandmother's bedroom. There was an old oil stove, which I tried to light, but to no avail. I left a dozen spent matches strewn on the floor. A clock on the dresser and another on the bedside stand had wound down and frozen at different times. *A stopped clock is right twice a day*, I remembered.

A single white sheet draped like a shroud over the bed's bare mattress. From a shelf in the closet I pulled down a pillow, two quilts, and a feather comforter, took off my shoes, and on top of the dusty sheet crawled beneath the blankets with my clothes still on. The sky outside the windows was still black when I fell asleep.

3

The whup-whup-whupping of a diesel tractor starting woke me. The sun was shining brightly in the half-bare branches outside, catching the flaming yellow of the remaining leaves and casting long shadows away from my window. Groggy, I yawned and stretched as I slowly figured out where I was and how I had gotten there. Out from beneath the comforters, the house was cold. I stuck my feet into my shoes, and without lacing them, stumbled out back to pee. The sunlight felt warm on my shoulders. I dug out my toothbrush and toothpaste and brushed my teeth at the pump, spitting the foamy residue into the grass. Then I pumped more cold water into the pitcher and washed my face in the wash bowl on the counter inside. I dried off on a dish towel hanging from a wooden peg. The waste water I carried outside and spilled on the lawn. Just like in the old days.

I stood in the warm morning sun and examined the smoke house behind the house. The unpainted boards had stained a dark maroon by decades of smoke and rain and sunlight. There was a padlock on the door. I had no idea where the key might be, and I didn't want to go in there anyway. I remembered the mud daubers and their nests that had scared me when I was a child. God knew what else might now be lurking inside.

I was hungry. But before I could do anything about that, nature called. I high-stepped through the dewy grass looking for the path to the privy in the cornfield out back. I found a mowed track through the yellow, brittle stalks, broken down and shorter than I remembered. At the end stood the outhouse, a tall, narrow structure once whitewashed, but now weathered to a dull gray. It seemed to lean a little toward the north. A forked stick in the hasp held the door shut. Inside, on the bench, lay a pile of old newspapers and a wrinkled roll of toilet paper. On the floor was a coffee can of lime with a rusty measuring cup inside. The two holes were covered with tin lids. I removed one, rolled up a piece of newspaper, and swirled it around inside to clear out the spiders. As I had been taught. Black widows, they had warned me. I had never experienced one, and didn't want to now.

As I relieved myself, I wondered why there were two holes. I couldn't imagine sitting there next to another person while he was doing his business. Maybe the two-holer was a kind of rural status symbol. The yellowing newspapers were years out of date and not of much interest. It was a trip back through time. Not just the newspapers. And not just my own childhood recollections. But to a time much earlier. To the early-Twentieth or the late-Nineteenth Centuries even. And earlier still. *This was how everyone once lived*, I thought. When I was done, a scoop of lime went down the hole before I replaced the tin lid. Just as I had been taught.

I strolled downtown to find a bite to eat. There wasn't much downtown left. Certainly no place to grab a sandwich. The old general merchandise store, Fingerhut's, was boarded up, and the empty building had that long-abandoned look of final surrender. Sharp's ice cream parlor was gone, too, though I couldn't place exactly where it had been. There was no drug store. The post office had been moved to a small prefab structure across the tracks, but still appeared to be doing business. Two pickups were parked out front and a car sat in back. The feed store across from it might have still been open, but I didn't see anyone moving around outside that morning.

The beer joint was not where it used to be. "A devil's lair," according to my grandmother's judgment. Then, I had believed her. Now, I frequented such places. The beer joint had relocated up the block inside the neo-classical facade of the old bank building on the corner. The once-proud monument to prosperity, progress, and hard work for this rural farming community had become the refuge of the local alcoholics and ne'er-do-wells. My grandfather had run that bank until the Depression had put him out of business.

Standing not far from the re-imaged bank was a small new building with red metal siding and two pumps outside, one for regular and one for diesel. A white sign read "Right Way Market." Inside was a small convenience store. The bell over the door tinkled as I went in. A slender young woman stood on her tip-toes behind the counter, reaching high over her head to restack the shelves with pints of liquor and packs of cigarettes.

"Howdy," I said.

"Hello," she replied without looking back. "Can I help you?"

"Looks like the town has changed since I was here last."

"Oh?" She turned with a little more interest. I towered over her. She might have been a few years older than me, but it was hard to tell. She had a pretty face, framed by long auburn curls pulled back in a ponytail. Her eyes were the color of pale tea. The suntanned arms reaching from her sleeveless blouse were well-muscled and shapely. I couldn't see her legs because of the full-pleated blue skirt. "You from around here?"

"I'm staying over at my grandmother's house."

"Oh? So who might your gramma be?"

I told her.

She smiled. "When I was a girl, I used to help Louisa out with the wash." She pronounced it "warsh", as my grandmother did. "Helped her with some of the other chores, too. Over at her place." Hers was a sweet smile. A welcoming smile. As if I just might belong to the local clan. "So how's Louisa doing these days?"

"Not so well," I said. I told her a little about the nursing home. The sounds. The smells. Grandmother's inability to recognize anyone. Her smile drooped, became a frown.

"What brings you here today?" she asked.

"Food," I said, deflecting the broader question. "Just picking up a few provisions for the day."

"Well, help yourself." She turned back to restocking the shelves. I watched her stretch lithely on her toes, admiring her grace

"How long's Fingerhut's been closed?" I asked her.

"Oh, that was quite a while back. Maybe five years. Maybe more."

"And the beer joint's moved to the bank?"

"Yes, sir. Ain't that somethin'? Who would've thought? That was a little after Fingerhut's closed."

The bell tinkled and a white-haired old gentleman in faded bib overalls and a Cardinals baseball cap hobbled in, favoring his left leg and leaning on a cane. He chatted with the clerk as he bought a pack of Camels. I looked around the shelves and collected a jar of peanut butter, a loaf of bread, a can of sardines, and a box of saltine crackers, which I set on the counter. I found a small box of Wheaties and a quart bottle of milk and added them to my cache. While she was still engaged with the old farmer, I pulled a six-pack of Falstaff out of the cold case, even though I was not nearly old enough to buy beer. I just thought I'd see what happened.

After the farmer limped out, she rang me up, not hesitating with the beer. She looked at me, but didn't ask any questions except, "Need a church key?" I nodded, and she tossed an opener into the bag. I handed her a five dollar bill, and she returned a one and some change.

I sorted through the coins, added a box of Cracker Jack to the bag, and handed her a dime. I was enjoying the fresh scent of her and didn't really want to go back to the empty house. "Does the train still run through town?" I asked.

"Sure does. Twice a week. My uncle used to be a brakeman for the MoPac, and–"

"Wait, wait, what's a 'mow-pack'?"

"That's what they call the Missouri Pacific around here. Anyway, he came through here workin' the Belmont Branch a time or two, when things were slow on the main line. Sometimes they'll still spot a car on the siding here." It felt like she was enjoying the conversation, too.

"I remember when the old steam engine used to come through," I said. "You remember it?"

"Sure I do," she laughed, her face bright. "Used to scare the dickens outta me when I was a little girl."

"Me too! I used to run inside and try to shut all the doors to keep the sound out."

We laughed together.

"What's your name?" she asked

I told her.

"Well, hi." She held out her hand. "I'm Joylene Crites."

"Pleased t'meet ya, Joylene Crites."

We prattled quite a bit more about Whitewater and growing up there, until the service bell rang and Joylene had to hurry outside to pump gas into a dilapidated old pickup truck.

I hoisted my bag of groceries and stepped outside, waving to her as I headed back up Main Street, feeling lighter than I had in days. I was a stranger in town. I could be anything. I carried no baggage. I could re-invent myself at will. I liked the sense of freedom. "Joylene Crites," I repeated out loud.

A cold wind had come up from the north, stripping the last of the autumn leaves from the bare branches. They floated and soared and danced in the stiff breeze, dry and brittle and yellow, before descending to rattle and scrape across the concrete sidewalk. High clouds were drifting in from the west, and by the time I climbed the porch steps, they had obliterated the sun. The gusts were cold. The whole damned house was cold. I set down my groceries in the kitchen and ate a bowl of cereal at the table with my jacket zipped and my collar turned up.

After breakfast I tinkered again with the stove in the bedroom and found that all I needed to do was go outside and twist open the valve on the oil tank perched on its tall wooden trestle. Then the stove lit easily. I closed the bedroom door to warm up the room. A light rain began to fall. Driven by the wind, it tapped and scratched its fingernails against the pane.

I wound both the clocks. Not knowing what the real time was, I set them both for twelve noon, and they began ticking away. Loudly. The metal escapement of the smaller clock on the bedside stand clacked against metal gears like a tiny pistol ejecting shell casings. The large mantle clock on the dresser had a deeper, more substantial voice. They ticked at different speeds. The timing was off. They were out of synchronization. It was an orchestra without a conductor. The alarm clock would match the mantle clock for a few beats, then move ahead like a runner pulling away on a circular track, until it ran precisely opposite, and the ticks would emphasize each another like the backbeat of a song. The small clock would then dash onward through a mechanical cacophony until it lapped the mantle clock and restored order to the universe for a few ticks. A complete lapping cycle took a couple of minutes, more or less. I didn't try to time it. Which clock would I use?

When I ran out of distractions, time brought me to the task at hand. To be a writer, I would have to write something. I punched open my first beer. I would write something simple and profound. A poem. Put the universe in perspective. I dug out a ball-point pen and my spiral notebook. The pages were all blank, waiting for my creation. It had to be something meaningful. Something to justify the ordeal of the long trip down here. Something like Kerouac might have written. I took a deep pull of Falstaff to lubricate the creative process, then leaned back in the wooden chair to wait for inspiration.

Nothing came. The clocks ticked, running their meaningless laps around and around inside my head. I finished my first beer and opened a second. I had to write something. *Anything.* The room had grown warm. The rain tatted against the window. Finally a phrase caught in my mind, revolving with the clocks. It changed and revised itself, adapting like a living thing. When at last it perched, I netted it like a butterfly and pinned it to the page.

The ticking, ticking of two clocks
Is different, for nobody knocks.

I looked at it dully, vaguely disappointed. I drained my second beer. Stood up and stretched. I was still hungry. So I went back into the kitchen, leaving the bedroom door open to distribute the warmth. I made a peanut butter sandwich and washed it down with another beer.

Returning to the bedroom, I left the door ajar and examined what I had written. *"Jesus!"* I muttered. *Is this the best I can do?* Discouraged, I kicked off my shoes, lay down on the bed, and rolled over. The warmth from the stove felt good. The air seemed thick and cozy. The rain scratched the back of the window pane. I thought of Joylene's beautiful smile. Her scent. The smoothness of her tawny skin. I fell asleep.

4

The bedroom was stifling hot. I rose from the bed, turned off the furnace, and stumbled out onto the front porch. The afternoon had grown gloomy. The rain had stopped, but a thick mist still settled over the wet grass. Fat drops pattered down from the bare branches onto the cold leaves strewn beneath them. In the damp air I could see my breath.

I turned back inside, punched open another beer, and rinsed out my mouth with the tepid foam. It was not refreshing, but I swallowed it anyway. I yawned and stretched and rolled my neck and arched my back and felt a couple of vertebrae pop into place. I had come here to find myself. To sort things out. To resolve some issues. But I couldn't even get my mind around what needed sorting out.

I lit the kerosene lamp in the kitchen, which made the afternoon seem even darker outside the windows. I opened the tin of sardines and ate them slowly with the crackers and beer. As the salty little dead fish grew harder to choke down, I had to open another beer. One Falstaff left. I was bored. Didn't know what to do with myself. Disappointed, somehow. This was supposed to be my big adventure. But I felt more like a rodent trapped inside a cardboard box.

I pulled on my jacket and strolled the two blocks over to the beer joint, thinking maybe I might run into Joylene. That would be nice. She wasn't there, of course. So I ordered a bottle of beer and drank it alone at the far end of the bar. At the other end two elderly farmers and the barkeeper were all drinking Falstaffs, but that was about all we had in common. A younger man came in, nodded to me, and joined the others with loud joking and backslapping. I felt invisible and uncomfortable, so I finished my beer and lurched back to the house.

I relit the furnace and tried to add a few more couplets to my poem. It was an ugly task. I managed to tack on another dozen lines, each one more lame and maudlin than the last, before I gave it up for good. This wasn't going at all the way I had planned.

5

It was already light when I crawled out of bed. The rain had stopped, but the sky was an ominous overcast that looked like it might bring snow. By leaving the bedroom door open and turning the furnace to its lowest setting, I had managed to establish a habitable balance. I went to the privy, washed up, and ate a bowl of corn flakes while I waited for the Right Way Market to open. When it finally did, I found a young fellow with greasy hair clerking there. I asked after Joylene. It was her day off, he said. She wouldn't be back for two days. I bought another six-pack of Falstaff, a jar of grape jelly, another tin of sardines, a can of Dinty Moore's beef stew, and two new batteries for the flashlight.

I couldn't find the stomach to reread my poem. Instead, I flipped the page over and stared at a fresh sheet. I stared at it for a long time. It seemed like hours. But nothing worth writing came to mind. I decided

I was pushing too hard, and set about finding something else to occupy myself. The sky seemed to be brightening, so I went out for a walk.

As I was eating a peanut butter and jelly sandwich back in the kitchen, I remembered an attic somewhere upstairs that had fascinated me as a child. I inserted the fresh batteries into the flashlight and climbed the steep stairs to explore the upper floor, pausing at each window to enjoy the view. I was just about to give up when I found the low half-door behind a hanging quilt at the back of the main upstairs bedroom. I pulled open the door and stuck my head and shoulders inside, holding the bright flashlight before me. I immediately came across a real treasure. An old crank telephone inside a polished oak box. Attached by a cloth-covered cord was a candlestick phone with a bell-shaped mouthpiece and a separate earpiece on the hook. Just like in the old-time movies. I dragged it out and examined it on the bedroom floor. Pleased, I crawled back inside to look for more. I beamed the flashlight across an old wooden chair with a needlepoint cushion under a dusty sheet. A wooden rocking chair. A box of women's clothes. A fishing rod. A dusty lamp with a rip down one side of the shade .

The doorbell rang. At least I thought I heard the old twist bell sound in the muffled attic. At first I wasn't certain I had heard anything, so I kept still. The bell rang again, loud and clear. *Jesus!* I thought. *What if it's the police! Come to see who broke in. What the hell am I going to tell them? Maybe I ought to just ignore it. Let them go away. But what if they didn't go away? Acting guilty might just make things worse.* So I crawled backwards to get out of that narrow space, and the bell sounded a third time as I extracted myself.

I thumped down the stairs and threw open the front door just as a short, graceful figure with an auburn pony-tail was closing the front gate.

"Hi," I called. "Joylene? Is that you?"

She turned, smiling. "Oh, I thought you weren't home." She wore a simple cotton dress with a pink flower pattern and a knit shawl over her shoulders. On her feet were penny loafers. She looked wonderful. "Is this a bad time?"

"No. Not at all. I was just crawling around in the attic. Would you like to come in?"

"Well," she stammered, as if reciting a practiced verse, "We didn't get a chance to finish talking at the store." Her cheeks were flushed. "And I hoped I could see the inside of Louisa's house again."

"Sure. Come on inside." I held the door.

I led her from room to room as she gushed with memories of when my grandmother still lived there. She seemed so small and animated and yet so perfectly proportioned. Each chair in every room she tried. In the front parlor dust puffed out when she bounced on the old horse-hair sofa. She told me about my grandmother and the joy she had felt helping her with the chores.

"Would you like to see the upstairs?" I asked.

"Oh, I don't think I've ever been up there. Yes."

I led the way up that steep stairway. "Watch your head at the top." We meandered through the narrow rooms. She looked out the windows and poked into the closets like a child. "This is a real feather bed," she laughed. "You sure don't see those much any more."

In the front bedroom I showed her the old telephone next to the open attic door.

"What else is in there?" she wanted to know, peering into the darkness.

"Let's go in. I haven't finished looking around." I handed her the flashlight and followed her inside. She poked around in the boxes, and I mostly watched her in the reflected glow of the flashlight. Her skin was clear. Her legs were slender and firm beneath that skimpy cotton dress. But mostly she seemed so happy as she remembered things from long ago. A long ago when things were somehow better for her.

After our leisurely tour of the house and attic, we stepped out on the front porch. The sun had come out and the afternoon was growing warm. We swung on the porch swing. The taut chains creaked and sang comfortably as we talked. She asked about me. I told her about the hitchhike down, and she seemed fascinated. She was a good listener and drew me out. I found myself talking about Bethany. I told her the whole damned story. And she seemed to understand.

"You'll meet somebody else," she said.

"I don't know," I replied. "I don't know . . . if I *can*."

"Oh, you can. And you will. Or somebody else will find you. You're too good a person. You'll see."

I went into the kitchen to fetch her a glass of water and came back with the six-pack of Falstaff. I tore one loose and held it out. "How about a beer?"

"No, thank you," she scowled. "I don't drink no more."

I nodded and set the beer down beside the door.

"My husband was a drinker," she said. "A mean one. Used to get ugly when he was drunk. Sometimes he'd slap me around pretty good. Sometime he even hit Molly."

"Molly?"

"Yeah. Our daughter. Her name's Molly. Molly Lynch. That's my husband's name. Lynch. Clyde Lynch. I changed mine back to Crites when we broke up."

"So you're divorced now?"

"Not actually divorced. 'Legally separated' is what they call it."

I thought about it. "Where's Molly now?"

"She's livin' over in Cape Girardeau with her gran'folks. Clyde's parents. His father's a big wheel in the county gover'ment over there. Clyde didn't want Molly. An' he didn't want me to have her. So they got legal custody. His parents. I'm supposed to have her sometimes. But I don't get to see her much anymore."

"How come?"

She just shook her head, looking like she might start to cry. She sucked in a deep breath and whispered, "Unfit mother." Slowly she stood, bracing herself against the wall, and stepped into the front hall. With her back to me I heard her say, "Molly'll be three next month."

I didn't know how to respond. This was all about the real world I knew so little about. The big world, not the *Ozzie and Harriet* world of make believe. I eased into the front hall behind her. She was sobbing quietly. My eyes were misty too. I didn't know what I was crying about. For the loss of her child. Maybe. For the loss of Bethany. That too. But mostly because of something I thought I had found. I stood there mute as those silly clocks went on lapping each other on their invisible ticking racetrack.

"I'm sorry," I said at last and reached out my arm to give her a supportive squeeze across her shoulders.

"Don't," she jerked, as if burned by my touch. Her wet eyes held a flash of anger.

"I'm sorry," I said again. "I didn't mean to–"

"I have to go," she announced abruptly, slipping past me through the door. I watched as she stepped down the broken sidewalk, through the gate, and out of my life. She left as the sun was setting and never looked back.

Long I stood there before closing the front door. In the parlor I sat on the horse-hair sofa wondering what had happened. And listening to those terrible clocks as they chewed away at the empty time I had left there in Whitewater.

6

By Wednesday morning the clocks had stopped. Wound down. Both of them. The silence was an eerie presence. Hollow. Like something was missing. Like someone had died. A profound sadness seemed to echo within that emptiness.

I packed my duffle bag, put the house back the way I had found it as best I could, and locked the doors, pushing the key back under the front door with a twig. I dumped my garbage in the trash barrel at the Right Way and returned the six-pack to the cold case inside. I didn't ask for a refund. I waited outside until a clean-shaven young man with a crew cut agreed to give me a lift back to Dutchtown.

I made it back to my aunt's house in Illinois for Thanksgiving dinner. Just barely. The rides that day were short and far between. All that night I stood waiting in the cold and dark for someone to pick me up. Folks don't pick up hitchhikers after dark. I arrived with the dawn and had to sleep while we waited for the rest of my family to arrive. It wasn't pretty. "What were you thinking?" "Do you have any idea what you've put us through?" "Don't you ever think of anyone but yourself?" But I had expected all that. It was part of the cost of doing business. I didn't have much to say in response.

I never heard from Joylene again. I tried to write her, twice, in care of the Right Way Market, but she never wrote back. High school dragged on and rushed by. Like two clocks ticking out the same time. Bethany moved in her circles, and I in mine. After graduation, she enrolled in a small Christian college in Minnesota, and I lost track of her.

Neal Cassidy would thrive into the 60s to become a Merry Prankster and acid freak in San Francisco, devoting himself to a life of partying, outrage, and madness. But by then I was already in law school across the Bay, ostensibly on track to becoming a productive member of society, and Berkeley was madness enough for me. In 1968 Cassidy was found unconscious along a lonely stretch of railroad track outside Guanajuato, Mexico. He died a few hours later of undetermined causes, probably alcohol and barbiturate poisoning. He was 42. Kerouac died the following year of internal bleeding caused by liver cirrhosis, the result of a lifetime of heavy drinking. He was 47.

In my imagination, I can still hear the ticking, ticking of those two clocks as they make their unsynchronized circles in the stuffy bedroom of that antique farmhouse. A farmhouse which has long since been bulldozed out of existence. Only now, looking back, I can see that there was a third clock circling that imaginary racetrack. Sometimes sprinting ahead. Sometimes lagging behind. Sometimes puzzling over what might come to pass. Sometimes poking around in the ruins of what once had been. Even as I am doing now. It was my own clock, of course. My internal time consciousness. My mind. And now that clock too is winding down.

With the perspective of over a half a century, I see that the trip to Whitewater changed the course of my life. Perhaps only in a small way. How does one judge, not knowing what the alternatives might have been? I think that the exercise in praying freed me to move on. As if, when I had finished, I could say to myself, "Okay. Now it's in God's hands. That's the best I can do. And if He can't – or if He *won't* – give me a break here and help me out, then fuck it, I'll just have to deal with it myself, as best I can." Perhaps that was the moment I began to think of God not so much as a Grand Puppeteer, but rather as a Master Clockmaker. A clockmaker who has created an instrument that now ticks along on its own without the need for further intervention. And in time I stopped thinking about God at all. That was the last time I ever tried to pray.

Gandy Dancer

Every mornin' at the mine you could see him arrive,
He stood six foot six and weighed two-forty-five,
Kinda broad at the shoulder and narrow at the hip,
And everybody knew you didn't give no lip to Big John
—Big Bad John, composed 1961 by Jimmy Dean and Roy Acuff

I didn't know much about real railroads back in the summer of 1961, except that I liked to watch the trains go by. They reminded me of the joy I used to feel as a kid running my Lionel in circles on the living room rug. But in 1961 I was a sophomore in college and looking for a summer job. I had already answered an ad for a brakeman on the Elgin, Joliet, & Eastern Railroad and had driven all the way down to the main office in Joliet for my pre-employment physical. A routine deal, they said. But they rejected me, claiming I was red-green color blind. I dispute it still, by god. There *was* no number in the last page of that little book of colored circles.

Anyway, I applied to the Chicago & Northwestern and landed a job on a track crew out of the yard in Waukegan, Illinois. "I'm gonna be a gandy dancer," I hummed to myself when I got my notice, although no one else uttered that archaic phrase any more. This was way back when the principal motive power on the C&NW, both passenger and freight, was the big EMD F7 units referred to as "streamliners" by the marketing staff and as "covered wagons" by the maintenance crew who had to crawl inside the cramped, airless space to service the 1500 horsepower prime movers. All I remember is my awe at those monsters, painted bright stagecoach yellow with dark green trim above, thrumming at idle in the main yard as the track crew assembled for work amid the sharp odor of creosote and diesel fumes. You didn't just hear that deep-throated rumble, you felt it in your bones. In your guts.

Our main task was to replace failing crossties along the passenger rails running north and south from the Waukegan yard. The bad ties had already been marked with yellow chalk by a track inspector. The passenger line was a double track running along the Lake Michigan shore plain just below the Sheridan Road bluff. The freight line lay out west by Highway 41, and our crew never had anything to do with that.

The foreman of our crew was Martinez. He was a small man. Small and tough. He knew how to do everything that needed to be done to maintain a railroad track. Martinez was able to show even us white boys, with our soft hands and sunburn-prone skin and heads full of Shakespeare, how to pry out a spike with the long pry bar, how to knock off a tie anchor with a single blow of the sledge hammer, how to lever out a broken tie with the lining bar, and how to tamp ballast with a fork until it was firm and stable. He had been assigned to foreman our track crew even though he spoke little English. A couple of the Mexicans on our crew could translate well enough to get the work done.

There were only three Anglos on the crew, all of us still in school. All of us were there for summer jobs, not careers. Marty, who had been a year ahead of me in high school, was in his third year at some big university back east that now escapes me. Maybe it was the University of Maryland. Someplace that held no significance for me. He was blond and slender with that pale skin that browns so nicely in the sun, but surprisingly strong and adroit. Marty was the only one on the crew, besides Martinez, who could actually hit the head of the spike consistently with the tiny face of the spike driver. I tried, but couldn't do it. Wielding a spike hammer seemed to me a skill you had to be born with. Being an upperclassman, Marty was a little aloof at first, but we soon became friends.

The other Anglo was Jules. Only in Spanish, you pronounced it "Yools." So he was called "Yools" all that summer. Yools . . . something. I can't recall his last name. Nor Marty's either, for that matter. None of us had last names. Ricardo. Marty. Yools. Manuel. Felipe. Others I can't recall. All except Martinez. Martinez was Martinez. All the rest of us were first names only.

Anyway, Yools was a big, quiet, red-headed guy I hadn't known before, because he graduated from Warren High School out west in Gurnee. He was a sophomore at Northern Illinois University. He did his work and kept to himself, so I never really got to know him. But Yools was the one we called on to help haul the really heavy stuff, like the long switch ties, or help lift the poochie cart on or off the rails.

The rest of the crew were all strictly from the railroad labor force. Latinos mostly. Career railroad men. None had finished high school, but we all got along together. The work unified us, and there were no slackers. They were all impressive workers, strong and muscular and fast and knowledgeable about railroads and adept at the use of the track tools. The Mexicans were friendly and laughed with Martinez in a language that we, as outsiders, could not fathom.

We began our work down along Market Street, in the "Negro" part of town with its rumors of pleasure and peril, where the track shot south from the Waukegan station yard, straight as an arrow for two or three miles, past St. Mary's Cemetery, until a broad curve swung it westward and out of sight. There we could see the headlight of a northbound locomotive coming for minutes before it arrived, the bright pinpoint of a silent, twinkling star where the parallel rails seemed to converge, which would grow and grow until it became a blinding pair of searchlights in the curved yellow face of steel that thundered down on us, shaking the ground, with its diesel roar and two-chime air horn blasting us out of the right-of-way. That stretch of track was our office and our workshop for the first few weeks as we crept slowly southward toward that blind curve that was to cause so much trouble later on.

I remember my first day on the job. It was already hot as the sun rose fiery above the lake. Hot and humid. My T-shirt was damp as I walked over to the crew in my heavy work boots, old levis, and brand new stiff leather gloves. I found Martinez and handed him my paperwork.

He glanced at it and said, "Ricardo." That was it. I had a new name for the rest of the summer. Martinez folded the papers and stuck them in his back pocket, then called out, "Get the poochie cart."

We followed a couple of the Mexicans past a huge stack of long, creosote-black switch ties to a small handcart sitting beside the rails of the mainline. Though small, the poochie cart was heavy with a steel frame and iron wheels with a two-by-six wooden deck painted yellow. It took all the strength of four men to lift it and turn it and set it on the tracks.

"What about the trains?" I asked someone. It was probably Marty.

"It's okay. Martinez's got a timetable. We take it back off if a train comes along."

And that's how it would be done the whole summer. There were no walkie-talkies in use then. You consulted the train schedule and kept your eyes and ears open to avoid conflict. The train crew knew we would be there, but they never slowed down. It was our job, and Martinez' responsibility, to keep the tracks clear for the regular passenger traffic.

So we loaded the poochie cart with jacks and bars and shovels and other tools I didn't recognize and a silver corrugated Igloo cooler of water and a bottle of salt tablets and began rolling south. The steel wheels grated rhythmically on steel rails with the crunch of bits of gravel between the two. And the smell of creosote was always with us. The smell of the railroad.

Before we were past the station yard limit sign, we came to our first tie marked with yellow chalk. Beyond it several more were marked. They appeared singly and sometimes in clusters, but the big yellow chalk mark was always the same. The new ties lay scattered along the side of the ballast, square-edged, black, and fragrant with creosote, where they had been tossed from a passing flatcar. We unloaded the tools and hauled the poochie cart off the mainline. The task seemed simple: remove the unsound tie and replace it with a new one. But we had to learn how to do it first.

Martinez and two burly Mexicans showed us how. They worked fast. First they knocked off the tie anchors. Then they pried out the spikes with a long bar that had a curved iron claw at one end. Then one man chopped at the ballast with a pick until the big chunks of crushed rock were loose enough to shovel into a pile on the adjacent ties and expose the bottom of the bad tie. A little more work with the pick and the tamping forks loosened the ballast underneath until the old tie dropped down away from the rail. A trench was dug in the ballast at the outside end of the tie and a lining bar on the other end pried the old tie out through the trench, where it was pulled out by hand and cast aside. A new, square, full-dimension tie, oozing creosote, was then plowed back into the trench, tie plates were set in place, and the tie was lifted by one man with a lining bar while the others tamped the ballast under it until it pressed the tie plate snugly beneath the rail. A little tapping with the sledge hammer lined up the pre-drilled holes in the tie with those of the tie plate, and then Martinez pounded home the spikes, three powerful blows of the spike driver to each spike in a graceful ballet of sweeping overhead arcs in which he never moved his hands from their grip on the butt end of the hammer shaft. Replacing a tie took only a few minutes and looked pretty easy.

But it wasn't easy. Not by a long chalk. I was quickly disabused of any romantic notions about being a gandy dancer. It was just plain hard work, and it lasted all day long. Eight long hours with a half-hour break for lunch. Long after my muscles were tired and strained and beginning to ache. The palms of my hands were sore and bruised from jamming the tamping fork into the ballast with all the force I could muster. The sun burned my arms where I had gotten creosote on them and the sweat had spread it. By early afternoon of that first day, I was resolved to quit. I just couldn't do the work. It was too goddamned hard, and I was too soft. I thought about dropping my tools and just walking off the job. Then I decided that maybe I could make it through one whole day. I would simply not show up the next morning. To hell with losing a day's wages. It simply wasn't worth it.

But I didn't quit. Not that day. Not the next. Not that first hard week, even though I couldn't stop thinking about quitting. Even though my hands swelled up and ached enough to keep me from sleeping at night, and when I did sleep I awoke worrying before first light. I didn't quit. I don't know what stopped me, but as time passed I was glad that I stuck it out. My hands toughened up, my muscles grew stronger, and I felt proud to be a railroad man. And a railroad man was fearless, I thought. I wanted to be strong and proud and fearless.

That was the summer a song called "Big Bad John" started playing on every radio until you couldn't get it out of your head, like the ceaseless clanking of a hammer on a steel rail. It told the tale of a powerful, reclusive mine worker who never said much, but when the chips were down, he didn't hesitate to sacrifice himself for his fellow workers. The lyrics hummed through my head as I arrived at the rail yard in the morning with the sun just getting its footing on the horizon. That was me. Big Bad John. Only a railroad man, not a miner. Or so I wanted to believe. Strong like Big Bad John. Fearless. I wanted to be fearless. A railroad man without fear of anything. Subsequent events of that summer, however, showed me how wrong that fantasy could be.

Anyway, when we finished replacing that first stretch of ties, Martinez called on the crew to straighten the track with lining bars. It was a ridiculously primitive process. He would walk maybe a couple hundred feet down the track and sight back along one rail. Then he would signal the crew, each of us carrying one of the heavy steel lining bars, to move toward or away from him to where he saw a bulge. There he would stop us with a hand signal, then point right or left. We would jab the points of our bars deep into the ballast beneath the rail and with a "heave . . . heave . . . heave" lever the track the direction he pointed. The track moved grudgingly, inch by inch, floating in the ballast, until Martinez would signal us to stop. Sometimes we had to lever it back a bit. When he was satisfied, he would walk away down the track and we would follow him to a new bulge. This would continue until he had eyeballed it all into line.

We didn't spend the whole summer on that stretch of track running south from the station yard. In the second month Martinez received orders for us to help two other track crews replacing a crossing up in Kenosha. We were packed into two vans and when we arrived, one lane of traffic had been closed and men with pneumatic jackhammers were busting out the pavement of a heavily used crossing. Our role was support, to get the job done as quickly as possible. We helped haul old ties out and new ties in and with rail tongs joined the centipede of men crawling forward with an impossibly heavy new section of mainline rail. We were there only four days, but we worked late each day and earned our first and only overtime.

When we came back Martinez repositioned us to the mainline north of the station yard, where more bad ties had been marked on both the northbound and southbound lines. There we found more shade from trees arching over the bluff. We crept northward for a mile or two before, near summer's end, we returned to finish the track running south toward that blind curve.

One week the lower echelon of the crew was diverted to weed

suppression on several industrial spurs north of the yard. That was a nasty job. Hot and filthy and toxic. We loaded the big pressure sprayer onto the poochie cart, poured in a half-gallon of creosote, filled the tank the rest of the way with diesel fuel, and pumped it up. The spray was deadly to anything growing into the right-of-way, and the blow-back would dampen your skin so that the sun would burn whatever skin was exposed. I remember one of the spurs leading to the tanning and rendering works, where the air was almost too foul to breathe. As I fought through the brush one afternoon, I was stung by wasps on the back of my hand a half dozen times, and my hand throbbed and began to swell. That night it swelled up like a cow's udder. I had to take the following day off until the swelling went down. That was the only day of work I missed that summer.

It stayed unseasonably hot and humid all that summer, with little rain. When it did rain, we worked anyway. We just got wet. But the merciless, unceasing sun burned us and sapped our strength. We swallowed a lot of salt tablets with our deep drafts of water from the Igloo cooler to replenish the sweat loss. By evening I was exhausted and my shirt could practically stand up from the film of dried salt caked on it.

Toward the end of summer I was feeling pretty proud of myself being a railroad man. Maybe a little too proud. Maybe a little too cocky. One afternoon, it must have been a Saturday as I recall, I was drinking beer with some of my non-railroad buddies at a bar down in Half Day. I was feeling pretty good and slid into a booth beside a pretty woman sitting by herself.

"Hi," I said.

We had chatted for only a minute when someone grabbed me by the arm, trying to pull me out of the booth. "What the hell are you doing here?" he demanded. His grip slipped and I felt my sleeve tear loose at the shoulder seam. "That's my wife," he yelled.

I stood up and faced him. He was about my age, about my weight, but I towered over him. "You tore my shirt," I told him calmly.

"Get the hell away from my wife. And stay away." He was seriously riled up.

"You tore my shirt," I repeated, still calm.

"I don't give a damn," he said.

By then my buddies had joined me. A few of his friends had drifted over too.

"You gotta pay for my shirt," I told him. Still calm. Still matter of fact.

"The hell I will."

The rest of the patrons had quieted down, watching the contest. Someone said the bartender was going to call the cops.

"You keep away from my wife." It was a big territorial deal for this guy. And I was on his turf.

But I didn't back down. Big Bad John wouldn't have backed down. Suddenly I roared at him, "I'm a railroad man! And I've driven spikes bigger'n you into the ground!" I didn't push him. Didn't touch him. I just added, "Let's go outside and settle this."

I walked out into the sunlight with my buddies and waited for him. The cops never showed up. After a while one of his friends came out with a couple of dollars for the shirt and I took them and we all left feeling pretty good about the whole thing. He refused to fight me, and that was fortunate. Looking back, I have no doubt that was a very fortunate thing.

Generally we avoided using the jacks when we replaced ties. A raised jack can derail a slow train and wreck a fast one. Where the rocky ballast sits above the grade of the right-of-way, as it does in most places we were working, you just had to dig out a trench on the outside of the ballast, drag the old tie out by its end, and shove a new one in. When a train came by during the process, you simply stepped back and waved to the engineer. But sometimes the track enters a cut, and in places like that where the ties are crowded in by the surrounding banks on both sides, that method isn't possible. Jacks have to be inserted beneath the inside mainline rail to raise it at least a foot so the ties can be dragged up and out across the adjacent track.

Toward the end of summer, as we resumed our march southward from the station yard, we came to just such a place at the north end of the cemetery where a spur ridge dropped down from the bluff toward the lake. The right-of-way had been cut through the ridge beginning about a quarter mile from the big blind curve and stretching north maybe a hundred feet. In that stretch a dozen ties had been marked for replacement with the yellow chalk mark now faded by the sun and rain and railroad traffic. Jacks would be required.

Martinez equipped Marty with a red flag on a short staff and a whistle and sent him on down to the curve. Marty was to station himself halfway around where he could watch the northbound track beyond and we could still see him. He would be able to see a northbound train coming for miles and signal us to let down the jacks.

Then Martinez divided us into three squads. He would lead one, and Felipe and Manuel, his corporals, he put in charge of the other two. I was in Manuel's squad, the furthest from the curve. We had to replace two bad ties, separated by two good ones.

We began as usual by pulling out the spikes and digging out the ballast beside and below the bad ties until they dropped free and the tie plates could be removed. The ballast was piled between the rails as usual. We carried two new ties and positioned them ready to go. I helped Manuel dig out the ballast below the inside rail between the two good ties. He pushed around the ballast until he had what he thought was a good base. Then he hauled over a heavy 15-ton ratchet-action railroad jack. The jack looked like an old style automotive jack, but heavier, big enough to lift a locomotive, and it could lift from either the top or from a foot on the side. He lowered it into the hole and shoved it under the rail for a test fit, making sure there was plenty of clearance. After fitting it, Manuel hauled it out again and laid it in the trough between the northbound and southbound tracks. Then we stepped back and waited for Martinez to consult his timetable. He waved for us all to move out of the cut while we waited for the 10:08 to come by.

Marty began waiving his flag, and a few minutes later the 10:08 rounded the curve like a flexible yellow bullet and thundered past, right on time. Martinez signaled us back to work, spinning his fist to hurry us along. We had until the 10:42 to get the old ties pulled out and the new ones shoved in. I watched as Manuel ploughed the jack rather clumsily back beneath the rail and worked the ratchet mechanism with his fingers until the foot rose several inches to catch the bottom of the rail. The top of the jack stuck at an angle above the rail. Then Manuel inserted a lining bar into the rachet mechanism and pumped it up until it reached its full extension. The rail and surrounding ties all came up together, except for the ones we were going to remove. The base of the jack had crunched down into the gravel, and Manuel stared at it. The rail had not come up as much as he expected. He knelt indecisively for a moment, then jumped up and motioned us to get to work. But things didn't go well. There were complications. Manuel had set the jack too low and the old ties stuck when we tried to pull them out across the adjoining track. The jack was all the way up, so he had no choice but to drop it down again and ordered us to find a shim. The tie was now jammed under the rail and sticking halfway out into the southbound track. Nobody could find a proper shim, but someone brought a couple of discarded, rusty tie plates. Manuel muscled out the jack and pushed some ballast back in with his gloved hand and placed the tie plates on top of the rock. One tie plate was too short, but two were too tall, so he had to adjust the ballast before forcing the jack back under the rail as the time ticked away. He pumped the jack all the way up again. Now we could pull the old ties free and toss them aside, but the new ones stuck and had to be sledge-hammered into the trench, plowing ballast before them. Martinez had to stop what he was doing to come over and give Manuel a hand. Manuel was sweating and feeling the pressure. When the new ties were in place, Manuel hurried up the slope and into the brush to relieve himself. This was long before portable toilets dotted every work site. Martinez inspected the clearances, judged them acceptable, then hurried back to where he had been working.

That was when someone finally remembered to look up and shouted, "*Train coming!*"

Marty was jumping up and down at the curve flapping and waving his flag like a flightless bird. You could see his cheeks pooched out blowing into the damned whistle that none of us had heard from that distance. But now we could hear its frantic scream woven into the background fabric of the city noise. No sooner had the cry arisen than the nose of the yellow streamliner swept around the blind curve hauling yellow cars filled with unsuspecting passengers.

"*Drop jacks!*" Martinez yelled and ran toward his jack. He and Felipe dove onto their faces to reach under the track to release the ratchet springs on the sides of their jacks. Then they heaved down on their lining bars and the rail settled back in place. They dug out their jacks and tossed them aside.

The third jack remained unattended. Manuel was still up in the bushes, and no one else stepped into the breach. No one knew how to lower the jack. We all stood there frozen.

The cars of the oncoming train were now in a line behind the locomotive and coming straight for us and growing and we could hear the engines thunder and the rising blat of the air horns as the engineer saw us and tried to clear the track. Sixty miles-per-hour and a quarter of a mile or less to cover between us. I did the math in my head. Fifteen seconds to drop the third jack, and no one was doing anything about it as the precious seconds evaporated. It was all happening fast, but my mind's eye was even faster. In a split second I foresaw the lead locomotive tipping horribly to the left, leaving the tracks, pitching over, and plowing through the ballast right where we were standing, the second locomotive jack-knifing the opposite way, and the passenger cars folding together like a broken accordion. Right where we were standing. The little valley exploding with crushed and crushing steel and spraying fuel while we stood there rooted like ducks in a shooting gallery.

So I turned and ran. The whole crew seemed to turn as one and run. I remember scrambling up the loose dirt of the cut bank with the lyrics of that stupid Big John song pounding in my brain. I know it sounds crazy, but sometimes it's those crazy little things that you remember that brings it back so vividly after all those years. I was scrambling away from a train wreck and feeling guilty about shirking my duty. I wasn't fearless. I was no Big Bad John. I was one of the scramblers trying to save my own sorry ass. And in my head the lyrics pulsed:

"Twenty men scrambled from a would-be grave and
Now there's only one left down there to save . . ."
Martinez!

I spun around and saw Martinez sprinting up the track ahead of the looming locomotive. He sprinted and dove and flopped on his belly on the ballast between the mainlines with the passenger train bearing down on him and he reached under the rail for the release lever on the side of the third jack. Everyone who had scattered had turned and were holding their breath. By then the engineer of the train had seen him and knew what was happening and knew that there was nothing he could do about it. With the horns rising to a steady scream, he notched down the throttle and applied the air brakes, which would have no chance of stopping the train with all its weight and momentum behind it. But I believe that the fraction of a second gained by applying the brakes slowed the train just enough to save Martinez and avoid the train wreck. Still on his belly, Martinez reached up and jerked down on the lining bar still stuck in the jack. As the train was on him and just before it eclipsed my view, I saw the rail sink down to its level position and Martinez roll away to keep from being sucked beneath the crushing guillotine of the wheels.

We heard the bang, clank, and zing of flying steel as the plow or maybe the leaf spring on the front truck smacked the top of the jack and lining bar, but the train never stopped. It slowed down, and after it passed without derailing, the engines racheted up again with plumes of black diesel exhaust. The passenger cars slipped past, one by ponderous one, while we waited. When the last car passed, we saw Martinez on his feet at the outside of the southbound track, brushing dirt and dust from his trousers as if nothing had happened. Business as usual. He had done what was expected of him. No big deal. But a shout went up from his crew. To us, he was a hero. He was Big Bad John.

We were converging on him, shouting and laughing, when Felipe, who was in the lead, held up his arms and turned like a traffic cop stopping traffic. Then we heard the blare of the horns of a southbound train approaching from the station yard, accelerating toward the blind curve where Marty was walking back with the flag drooping from his arm. As the train thundered between the crew and Martinez, I saw that the jack had been knocked on its side in the ballast beneath the rail. The impact had mangled it. The lining bar was nowhere to be seen. A railroad mainline is a dangerous place to work.

Martinez was uncomfortable with all the attention. He broke free from the huddle and signaled for Marty to go back to his position on the curve, then began yammering orders about "trabajo" and "andale," which I had learned meant "work" and "hurry up." We had a job to finish. Ties had to be raised and ballast tamped in place. Spikes had to be driven. And then would come the loading of the poochie cart and the long walk back to the yard.

That summer ended too soon. As all summers do, I guess, when you're young. I never returned to railroad work, except for building and maintaining a harmless G-scale garden railway in my back yard. A half-century has passed since I witnessed Martinez' heroics. A half century in which I finished my schooling, pursued a career as an attorney, and entered retirement at last. But I still recall it all. Martinez. Big Bad John. And the train wreck that never happened.

The Ride

I remember that day as bright and warm. Hot, actually, for so late in October. I was sitting by the side of a road out in Iowa somewhere. U. S. 30, as I recall. A backroad paralleling the interstate fifteen miles to the south. It cut through the cornfields connecting Cedar Rapids and Clinton and a whole lot of other towns and cities. But those two were the important ones. Cedar Rapids was behind me. Clinton lay ahead. I was heading east toward the bridge over the mighty Mississippi at Clinton. Actually, I was going all the way to Chicago, but crossing the big river was about all I could wrap my mind around just then. One step at a time, as they say.

For the past few days I had been hitch-hiking around, trying to get my mind right. Trying to escape from the life I was stuck in. School. Parents. Friends. I needed to take some deep breaths. Clear my head. Do some serious thinking. And drinking. The night before I had spent in a cheap hotel in downtown Cedar Rapids with a pint of bourbon to keep me company. I hadn't done a whole lot of thinking there. Now I was heading home. It was early afternoon, but I was already half-drunk. Still working on the bottle from the night before.

The sun blazed down on the highway as it stretched straight and flat through the corn stubble toward the west. Where I'd come from. In the distance it looked like water puddled on the road. A mirage. But no rides. To the east, more puddling. More stubble. No cars coming from that direction either. I lay back in the grass and pulled over my small duffle bag. Zipped it open. Out came my bottle, flashing in the sunlight. Only a half-inch of the amber liquid sloshed in the bottom. *Ah well.* I tipped it to my lips, heard the gurgling, felt the burn, and the bourbon was all gone. I lobbed the empty at a rock, but missed. Rolled onto my side, squinted west, and waited for some cars to come by.

It wasn't long before I spied a speck growing in the hazy distance. Other specks followed. Cars always seemed to come in spurts along country roads. I groaned and struggled to my feet. It took forever for the specks to grow into real cars and come within range. I lifted my thumb and jabbed it toward Clinton.

"Well *goddamn*," I muttered when I saw that the first car wasn't going to stop. I snapped in my thumb and stuck up my middle finger. Two more cars and a big chrome-grilled pickup followed, but one after another they whizzed past, each receiving my coarse benediction. The pickup blatted its horn.

When they were all gone, receding into the distance like forgotten promises, I sat down heavily, muttering. "No-good sonofabitches wouldn't pick up Jesus if he was bleeding in a ditch."

The sun went behind a small white cloud, but reappeared shortly. A dry breeze whisked across the stubble of corn fields lining the road. It bore the rich, earthy, almost sweet aroma of agriculture. Manure. Fertilizer. Maybe a hog farm upwind somewhere. Far in the distance a red barn shimmered, faded pastel by the haze. A silo loomed beside it, its dome glinting in the sun. A windmill blade turned lazily on its rusty trestle tower. Coming and going on the breeze an unseen tractor growled, endlessly churning the sea of loam. The day was too pleasant to remain mad. I felt warm and tingly all over. I got up, shouldered my pack, and started walking toward Clinton. Found a long stick and began drumming on the pavement in time to "Red River Valley."

". . . *For they say you are taking the sunshine–*"

I didn't hear the car until it was almost on me. I spun around. A rusty red old beater was bearing down fast. I threw out my arm and thumbed eastward.

The car slammed on its brakes and slid to a dusty stop on the shoulder fifty yards down the road. It was a faded four-door sedan. Maybe a Chevy. Someone had prepped the roof and trunk for repainting, but given up. The car had seen hard use.

I jogged up to the passenger side, where the window was already rolled down. A thick arm with a tattoo of some unidentifiable woman on the deltoid, half-covered by a tattered gray tee-shirt, rested against the passenger door. A puffy face beneath a short blond crewcut cranked back toward me. "Where y'headed?" he asked.

"Clinton." I said, panting a little.

"Got a drivers' license?" he asked, a little thick-tongued. "A valid one?"

"Sure," I said. "Illinois."

"Great. Throw your bag in back an' go on around and climb inta the driver's seat. Earl here's gonna let y'drive."

"I ain't lettin' *no*body drive," I heard the driver growl. Earl. "*I'm* drivin'."

"Aw, come on, Earl." Crewcut turned back inside. "I thought we *talked* about this."

"*You* talked about it." Earl's growl notched up a pitch. "*I* didn't talk about it. *I'm* drivin'"

"Then why'd ya *stop* for him?"

"Cause y'told me to, ya dumb ass."

They lowered their voices in a private row while I stood alongside the road, gazing off across the corn fields. A hawk circled in the distance. Looking for lunch. I couldn't make out what they were saying.

Finally crewcut turned back to me. His face was flushed. "Ya still wanna ride?"

"Sure," I said, but without conviction. Better than dying on this godforsaken highway.

"Jump in back then." Quietly he added, "We still might need ya t'drive."

I wrenched open the back door and tossed in my duffle, then climbed in over some empty beer cans, potato chip bags, and fast food detritus. The car reeked of stale beer, grease, and sour sweat. A cardboard box was tilted over the hump of the drive shaft. In it were a bottle of motor oil, a greasy rag, spark plugs and ignition parts, and some rusty tools. I shoved it over behind the driver.

"Thanks," I said, slamming the door.

Crewcut swivelled his head and nodded. Earl just stomped on the accelerator and popped the clutch. The car almost stalled, sputtered, coughed, then lurched forward, the back wheels spitting out gravel before squealing onto the pavement. Earl seemed to be in a big hurry.

The car was filthy, with oil stains and dirt on the floor, the seats, and even on the roof and walls. The two men in front didn't look much cleaner, and I sensed an uneasiness between them. Earl, the driver, appeared to be in his late twenties. Maybe thirty. He was short and thick with greasy black hair and a dark, round, unshaven face that sported an ugly little patch of beard on his chin. His collarless black tee-shirt revealed some sort of strange hieroglyphic tattooed on the side of his neck. He gripped the wheel with both fists.

Crewcut hooked his arm over the seat and regarded me with rheumy eyes. He looked to be a little older than Earl. Early thirties, maybe. He had a puffy, unhealthy look. His nose was sunburned and starting to peel, his eyes set a bit too close together. "I'm Butch, an' this here's Earl," he said, nodding to the driver.

Earl grumbled a greeting I didn't catch as the car shuddered through the speed limit and beyond. Dry wind blew into my eyes through the open window.

"Whach'*ur* name?"

"Bubba," I lied. I don't know where *that* came from. Just sort of popped out of my mouth. I didn't want to give them my real name. And "Bubba" felt kind of right. Like it might foster a little camaraderie.

"Don' look like no 'Bubba' t'me," Butch said. "If'n y'don't mind my sayin' so, ya'look a little . . . young for a name like that. Y'know . . . ya'look a little . . . *fancy*."

"I'm tryin' t'grow into it," I explained.

"Where're y'headed?"

I explained that I'd been goofing around for a few days and was now on my way back to school.

"Y' goin' t'school?"

"Yeah. Viet Nam, y'know. Tryin' t'avoid the draft with a 2-S deferment." I don't think he knew what a 2-S deferment was. "How 'bout you an' Earl? Been t'Nam?" I was easing into the dialect. Bonding.

Butch and Earl both snorted. "They ain't in'trested in our kind," Earl said, grinning and taking his eyes off the road for longer than I felt was prudent.

"We both just got outta the Linn County jail," Butch explained.

"Jus' this mornin'," Earl added.

Butch caught his eye, then confirmed, "Yeah, jus' this mornin'."

"What were y'in for," I asked, practicing the patois. "If y'don't mind my askin'.'"

"Me for drunk'n disorderly. Earl here for driving on a suspended license. Mine was took away way back."

That was sobering news. I glanced out at the cornfields blurring past. "So y'met in jail?"

"Naw. Earl'n me go way back. We're on our way t'Clinton t'see some hot gals we know. Gonna have us a real party." That seemed to remind him of something, and Butch reached under the front seat and pulled out a pint bottle. It looked about half full. He unscrewed the cap and tipped it to his lips. "Earl?" he said, holding the bottle out to the driver.

Earl grabbed it. Took a long swig. Handed it back. It was now a quarter full.

Butch was screwing the cap back on and was bending forward when a more hospitable thought crossed his mind. "Bubba?" He offered the bottle over the seat. "Want a swig of rot-gut?"

"Why not?" I wasn't feeling quite so mellow as before. My own buzz was riding the down elevator, but I was beginning to suspect I might need my wits about me before long. I twisted off the cap, raised the pint to my lips, and held it there for a moment, but took only a token sip. It burned like rat poison. I coughed and sputtered. Studied the unfamiliar label. "I agree," I wheezed, passing the bottle back. "That *is* rot-gut."

Butch was laughing. "Hey. Why pay more jus' t'get drunk?"

The corn fields rushed past. The car rocked and rattled. Sped through the hot afternoon. I squinted against the breeze. Earl kept the pedal to the floor as he tried to hold the left front wheel on the center line of the road, but it was too much for him. The speeding vehicle drifted back and forth. First into the eastbound lane. Then across the fog line and back. Then into the oncoming lane and back. Thank god traffic was light.

Silos rose up in the distance. And a water tower. A couple of white frame buildings. We were approaching a small town. In a while a "Speed Zone Ahead" sign flashed past. It didn't look like Earl saw it.

Suddenly a slow moving tractor appeared in the lane ahead, growing fast. Its huge tires rose like water wheels, the right one on the grassy shoulder, the left spinning well out onto the highway. Earl didn't seem to notice. I yelled something. Earl swerved. The car started to fishtail, but he managed to wrestle it back under control as we just missed smacking into the tractor.

"*Earl! Jesus! Y'gonna get us all kilt!*" Butch hollered.

"I gotta piss," Earl replied sullenly, as if that explained everything. "Stoppin' at the next gas station."

Butch turned to me. "Can y'drive stick?"

I nodded, my heart racing. Thinking it might be best for me to abandon ship and catch another ride.

"Y'got any money?"

"Just enough t'get me home."

"How 'bout a couple of bucks for gas?" His beady eyes were mirthless. Squinting. "We givin' you a ride an' all. Don't that seem fair?"

I fished in my wallet and pulled out two dollar bills. Handed them to him. Those were the days when you could still fill your tank for two bucks.

Well into the speed zone Earl slowed down and turned into an Esso station. He managed to bring the car in at an odd angle beside the pumps, jammed it into first, and was out the door before the wheels had stopped turning. "Let the kid drive," he muttered as he hightailed it for the outside door of the men's room.

When Earl was done, I followed him into the bathroom. Butch was pumping gas. Then Butch took his turn. They both went into the office while I eased myself into the driver's seat, barely pulling my legs under the steering wheel. I felt for the release lever and slid the seat back as far as it would go. Heard a corrugated crunch from the box I had shoved behind the seat. I turned the key and cranked up the engine. Tested the H of the gearshift with the clutch pushed in. Stared at the "R C Cola" sign in the window of the building. Waited. Not really drunk any more, I took a few deep breaths to clear my head.

It seemed to be taking a long time inside for fellows in such a hurry, but soon Butch and Earl were trotting back to the car. Butch piled in front. "Let's go," he grunted.

"Time's a'wastin'," Earl added as he jumped in back. I eased out the clutch and steered onto the highway. In back I could see Earl building himself a little nest in the trash. He soon settled in with his head against the window and closed his eyes.

The speed limit was 55, and I kept it below 60. Didn't want a ticket. The pace seemed glacial compared to Earl's aggressive pace, but no one said anything about it. Butch just stared silently out the windshield. Sort of dazed. Earl had dozed off. I was still a little tipsy, but unconcerned. I'd driven a lot drunker than this.

I remember rolling on for what seemed like a long while, down the arrow-straight blacktop dividing the corn fields, and then coming to a yellow curve sign advising 45 miles per hour. Not knowing the road, I slowed down. No complaint from my compatriots. The highway curved into a grove of trees, some still with tattered reds and oranges of autumn leaves, but most with ghostly bare branches glowing yellow in the sun. We descended to cross a short culvert bridge spanning a stagnant brown stream, then arced back up to the everlasting cornfields on the other side. I caught a glimpse of two black cars parked in the shade of the trees. They looked like Iowa Highway Patrol, and I was glad I had slowed down.

As I crested the rise I saw a flashing light in the distance. Straight down the highway maybe a mile or two. I eased up on the gas. Butch was in his own world and didn't seem to notice. I'd covered maybe half the distance when lights flashed in my rearview mirror. Those Iowa State Troopers were closing fast. Both of them, side by side blocking both lanes. Probably heading for the emergency lights ahead. Maybe an accident. I slowed even more and squeezed to the right to let them around, but they fell into formation right behind me. A siren began to wail. That got Butch's attention.

"What the hell's goin' on?" he wanted to know, craning to look out the back window.

I let up on the gas and looked for a place to pull over. The Troopers slowed to match my pace. The flashing light ahead, only a half mile away, resolved into the pulsing bubble on top of a black-and-white car parked across the road. Blocking both lanes.

Earl's head popped up in the rear view mirror, his eyes sleepy.

"Cops'r pullin' us over, Earl." Butch said. "What're we gonna do?"

"Jus' hold on." Earl replied, waking up. Thinking it through.

I found a wide spot and crunched slowly onto the shoulder and stopped. Clicked off the ignition. "I wasn't speeding."

One Trooper pulled off about fifty feet behind us. The other cruised past and pulled off the same distance ahead. They sat in their black cars, red lights spinning in bubbles on top. The black-and-white approached from ahead, light flashing. Not a State Trooper car. It pulled even with the Trooper in front, then angled onto the shoulder on the far side. I could read "Clinton County Sheriff" on the emblem on the door. All three sat with their red lights rotating silently. Menacingly.

"What'er we gonna *do*, Earl? I ain't gonna go back t'prison."

"Looks like we don't got a whole lot'a choices here," Earl replied.

"What about the gun?"

Gun? What the hell were they talking about a gun.

"Maybe they won't find it," Earl said. "An' if'n they do, we jus' tell'em it belongs t'Bubba here." I looked into his eyes in the rear view mirror. They were awake and sober now. Calm. Calculating. The eyes of a cornered animal. "You okay with that Bubba?"

I said nothing.

"Can't have no gun in *our* possession," Butch whined. He was pleading to me. "Neither one a'us. We' both ex-felons."

As if on cue, a uniformed man climbed out of each state police car, guns drawn, eyes focused on us. Their pistols were gripped seriously in both hands and pointed skyward. The sheriff's deputy wriggled out of the passenger side of his patrol car. The safe side of his black-and-white. He stood cradling a shotgun across his chest.

"Step out of the car with your hands up!" the Trooper in front commanded. He was the older of the two. The one in charge. He wore a chocolate brown shirt and matching Smoky the Bear hat. Tan trousers with a crisp black line tracing the seam. Serious black shoes gleaming in the sunlight. The vision burned into my retina like a Kodak snapshot.

I reached for the door handle, but Butch grabbed my right arm. "You'd do that for us, Bubba?" Butch begged, staring at me with sad dog eyes. "Tell'em its *yours*. Wouldn't ya?"

I jerked the door handle and shouldered it open, pulling free of Butch's grip. Fast enough to get free. But slow enough not to get shot by the Troopers. I stood with my hands spread above my shoulders and stepped away from the car toward the Trooper ahead of me.

"Down on the ground," he barked. "On your face. Arms out to the sides. Legs spread."

I complied, dropping in front of the car. The gravel bit into my knees. My palms. My cheek. I waited, pulse racing. Nothing happened. I lifted my head a few inches and saw the Trooper concentrating his full attention on the car. I was now under control. An afterthought.

What were Butch and Earl going to do? I began to fear that Butch might slide over and start the car. Run me over. Or jump out brandishing his hand gun. I didn't want to be laying there while a shootout raged above me. But there didn't seem much I could do about either possibility. My mouth was dry. My stomach felt hollow. My armpits sweaty.

"Officer?" I finally said.

He kept his eyes on the car. Didn't reply.

"Do you mind if I come on over a little closer to you?"

No reply.

"Those fellas kinda scare me," I added.

"Come on over," he said. "But keep your hands where I can see them."

I crawled. The sharp teeth of the gravel bit into my hands and knees.

"That's close enough," he said when I was within ten feet. I dropped to my belly again.

"You're not with them?" he asked softly.

"I was hitchhiking. They picked me up."

"But you were driving."

"Just started. Earl was drunk. Asked me to take over."

"Earl *Templeton*?"

"Didn't say his last name. Has weird tattoos on his neck."

The Trooper eased himself backward three slow steps. Around the hood of the cruiser. "How many with him?"

"Just one. Calls himself 'Butch.'"

"Butch *Sturka*?"

"Didn't say."

"Are they armed?"

"Butch said they have a gun," I said. "I didn't see it. I have no idea what they plan to do."

He thought about it for a moment, then called over to the sheriff's deputy. "Carl, I got one for you. Says he was just a hitchhiker."

Carl didn't come out from behind the black-and-white. He was no hero. A survivor. "Send him over, then."

"Get on over across the road," the Trooper said to me. "Keep your hands in sight and back on the ground when you get there."

I scrambled to my feet and crouch-ran across the highway with my arms sticking out to the side. Fell on my face behind the sheriff's car.

"Hands behind your back." Deputy Carl knelt down and clicked handcuffs onto my wrists. They bit into the flesh. Hurriedly he patted my pockets. "Don't move," he ordered, returning to his vigil. He was middle aged and frowning. Not a happy camper. Maybe a little mean of spirit from years in a tough job. He wore a wrinkled blue uniform. No hat. He laid the shotgun across the car roof and waited.

The minutes dragged on. Tense minutes. Everyone held their ground. A siren approached in the distance. My stomach churned acid. Dust tickled my nostrils. My wrists hurt. My fingers were going numb. But this didn't seem like my time to complain.

The siren grew louder. I twisted my head and saw another car approaching from the east. Another black-and-white. Its imminent arrival seemed to precipitate matters.

Things happened fast. Butch exploded out through the passenger door, running away from the road, stubby legs pumping. He was surprisingly fast.

"Stop right there," the old Trooper in front yelled. "Stop or I'll shoot!" He leveled his pistol at the fleeing man.

The younger Trooper from behind took off after him. Through the stubble. He was slim and blond and agile, leaping from row to row like a dancer. Butch saw him over his shoulder and spun around, a silver pistol in his right fist. The young Trooper dove for the ground as Butch fired a single shot. The pop was like a firecracker. The bullet must have flown over his head. The older Trooper fired two rounds from his position by the cruiser, pop, pop, missing with both, and Butch swung his pistol toward him. I jerked at a deafening explosion over my head. Deputy Carl had fired his shotgun. Butch bent forward and grabbed his belly with his left hand. I heard the click-clack of Carl's pump action. Butch tried to raise his pistol arm, but Carl blasted again, and Butch crumpled to his knees in the cornfield. He shook the pistol off his finger and clutched his face. His other hand still held his gut. "You bastard!" he screamed. "You blinded me!" The young Trooper hit him with a flying tackle. Knocked him over like a bowling pin. There was anger in that tackle. Guess he didn't like being shot at. The young Trooper wrestled Butch's right arm away from his face and twisted it behind his back, snapping on the cuffs. Then the left arm from his belly. Pushed him back into the dirt. Butch was crying and screaming insults, blood dripping from his face. From his eyes. Blood soaked the front of his T-shirt. The pistol lay on the ground beside him, gleaming in the sun.

I had to look away. Not because of the queasiness in my stomach, but because I was embarrassed for him.

A second black-and-white screeched to a stop beside Carl's cruiser. A young deputy jumped out of the passenger door. Same blue uniform as Carl's, but crisper. Captain's cap. A shotgun in his hands. He pumped a shell into the chamber.

"Call for an ambulance," Carl told the driver.

My ears were ringing from the shotgun blasts. No one paid any attention to me. They were all now concentrating their firepower on the car. I managed to squirm into a sitting position for a better view.

"Earl Templeton!" the older Trooper called out. "It's over! Come on out with your hands above your head!"

No response.

"Otherwise we will assume you are armed!" he added ominously.

"I'm coming out," Earl yelled. The back door on the passenger side clicked open and slowly swung wide. "I'm unarmed." His hands rose above the roof. Slowly he stood up. The old Trooper and the young deputy approached warily, got Earl Templeton on his face on the ground, and handcuffed him. They led him into the back door of the new black-and-white.

Well, I was thinking, *Earl got what he wanted. Someone else to take the fall for the hand gun.*

The ambulance came. Drove right out into the cornfield. They loaded Butch inside and drove off, siren wailing. The highway was reopened, and a slow stream of cars and trucks inched past, awe-struck faces gawking out the side windows.

"I can't feel my hands anymore," I told the old Trooper as he ambled by. He was gray at the temples. His face lined and wrinkled from too much wind and sun. Probably thinking of retirement soon. His wide-spread eyes tilted down on the outside, giving him an expression of permanent sadness. Or perhaps compassion. I hoped for compassion.

He regarded me. "Carl," he said to the deputy nearby, the deputy who had fired his shotgun. "I think we can take these cuffs off for now."

Carl came over and released the handcuffs. Hooked them onto his belt. Blood surged back into my fingers. Pins and needles. My hands burned as I rubbed them.

"Shake 'em," Carl said. "Like this."

I shook them.

The Trooper was still regarding me. He asked for my ID. I gave him my driver's license. He made notes on a clipboard. Handed it to Carl. Carl took a look and handed it back to me. "How'd you end up with this bunch?" Carl asked.

I told him I was hitchhiking.

"What the hell'er you doin' out here?"

I made up a story about visiting my sick aunt in the hospital in Cedar Rapids. "I'm on my way back to school. Have classes Monday morning."

"Where're y'going t'school?"

I told him where.

"That's a good school," said the Trooper. "Got a student ID?"

I fumbled it out of my wallet. Handed it to him. They both looked at it.

"Keeping y'out of the draft, is it?" Carl asked.

That caught me off guard. It seemed like a touchy topic, under the circumstances, my not knowing what his persuasion was. I decided to stick to the truth. "Yeah. 2-S deferment."

He thought about it and I got lucky. "I got a boy 'bout your age. A little younger. Still a senior in high school. I'd like t'keep him out."

I nodded. Waited.

"Don't get me wrong. I served my country. But that was between wars. This Viet Nam thing is another kettle of fish. It's a crazy mess. I don't want my boy going off over there. Maybe a 2-S would keep him out."

"Depends on his draft board," I said.

"Yeah." He thought about it. "Not a lot of fellas going on to college from Clinton High. Plenty a' cannon fodder. Guess that improves his odds. "

I waited while they conferred with the other Trooper and sheriff's deputies. A detective in a wrinkled sports coat was talking to them, taking notes, while a photographer flashed pictures of the bloody spot in the cornfield. They searched silently through my duffle bag on the patrol car hood, found nothing of interest, and zipped it back up.

Carl came back over and held my duffle out to me. "They say the gun is yours."

I shook my head. "I never even saw the gun, until . . . "

"Didn't think so. Those boys used it t'hold up a coupla gas stations back outta Cedar Rapids. Just the two of 'em, according to witnesses. One silver pistol."

The older Trooper rejoined us.

"Wh'da'ya aim t'do with him?" Carl asked him.

The Trooper shrugged. "Your call."

"You're not interested in haulin' him in?"

"Might save us some paperwork not to."

Carl grunted. "God knows there's gonna be enough paperwork the way it is."

"Your call," the Trooper repeated.

"The DA might need'im t'testify."

"Probably not. If he does, we know where to find him."

Carl thought about it for a while. An eternity, it seemed to me. "Aw, let'im get on back t'school. He didn't have nothin' t'do with this."

The Trooper nodded imperceptibly.

Carl turned on me. Searched my eyes. "I hope you learned something here," he said. "I hope t'god you got the message."

I had. And he saw it in my eyes. He smiled. "Come on, then. I'll give you a lift into Clinton. You won't be catchin' a ride here. Not with this peep show goin' on."

I rode in front with him. Neither of us spoke much. We each had our own thoughts to chew on. Like how it felt to shoot a man in the face. And how close I had come to blowing my college career. To carrying a rifle through the jungle. Not the kind of thing to talk about to a stranger.

He took me all the way across town to the west end of the long suspension bridge over the Mississippi River. Dropped me off. "Good luck," he said as I climbed out.

"Thank you," was all I could reply.

I decided to walk across the bridge. With my shadow lengthening before me, I stared down at the swollen, muddy water. It was dark and turbulent. Thinking isn't always something you do. Sometimes it just happens. I couldn't help thinking about Butch. Gut-shot. His face bleeding from the buckshot. I wondered if he would ever see again. Whether he deserved what he got. I thought about Earl and those cunning, merciless eyes. And what he deserved. What any of us deserves.

I haven't thought about either of them for years now. I remember that the walk was very long, but I made it across.

Pookie

"IT'S PIZZA AND BEER T-I-I-I-ME!"

Pookie's nasal whine echoed up the stairwell from two floors below. The entire slumbering fraternity house seemed to shudder awake to a sultry autumn afternoon brimming with sunlight and desire. Laughter skittered through the corridors. Then a devilish young man in white shorts and a madras shirt paraded his date past my open bedroom door. I tried not to glance up, but it was beyond my power to resist. The barefoot feline figure wearing a bright sun dress that dangled by thin spaghetti straps from her tanned shoulders quickened my pulse. A second couple followed on their heels, teasing and ribbing one another. Then a third. No one bothered to glance inside at me as they giggled past.

I turned back to my darkened cave trying to finish the odious reading assignment for Monday's sectional philosophy exam. It was 1962, the apex of the Parseghian Era at Northwestern University, and only a week before the opening football game. And I was putting my notes in order. That they were on Hegel's *Logic* raised a humorless smile. Hegel would be the first to agree that *someone* must stay behind and maintain order, after all.

I listened to the party rattle down the reverberating stairwell until the heavy steel fire door slammed shut at the bottom with the irreversible *ka-thud* of a sarcophagus lid. The house grew still and silent, but the silence made it even harder to wade through the metaphysical bullshit Hegel had scrawled down two centuries earlier. Then through the open window I heard laughter in the dusty parking lot and the cars starting and the crunch of dry gravel and the roar of each vehicle as it sped away. I stood up, stretched, and stepped to the window to look down. Everyone had gone. Dust was settling on the only car remaining in the lot, my old blue Ford coupe.

It was all so bitterly unfair. Hegel would have been hard enough to follow on a dark, somber midnight of winter, when snows locked a frozen world, but with weather this fine, the madman's interminable arguments were pure torture. The others didn't seem to give a good goddamn about exams. It was the same to them whether they passed them or skimmed by on probation. They were here to party.

Maybe they would wait for me at the pizza joint, my mind gnawed. *Maybe I could catch up.*

But I knew I would not. Certainly not without a date on my arm, and I could think of no immediate prospects. Muffy maybe. Probably not. A vision condensed of a stout young woman with dark, bristling hair. A smothering figure I wasn't even sure I liked.

Anyway, I needed to ace this test to improve my chances of getting into law school. So I eased myself down into the chair, angry with Hegel and the Hegelian world and the injustice of it all. Distractedly I compared my notes to the offensive treatise still open beneath the lamp. Dialectic. *Check.* Thesis. *Check.* Antithesis. *Check.* Synthesis. *Check.* Like the interminable clicks and whirs of a soulless calculating machine, Hegel's tedious German intellect trundled blindly toward its preposterous conclusion: *The real is the rational, and the rational is the real.*

"That's absolute bullshit!" I growled, slapping shut the offending volume. German Idealism was an incomprehensible universe unto itself, and Hegel's ponderous dialectic shuttled through a mad labyrinth of lofty words and bootstrap constructs, trying to prove the unprovable. *Reason! Rationality! Spirit!* It was an empty house of cards. An island built of syllogisms, but with no connection to the mainland. The heartbeat of reality was undetectable beneath the cloak of his thickly woven proofs.

And look where it had gotten the Germans. Karl Marx. Hitler. Even a lowly undergraduate like me knew better than that. Instead, Hegel *should* have written, *"The real is insoluble in reason, and any attempt at comprehension is futile. Live with it!"*

I turned my back on the crusty German philosopher. Angry and brooding, I pulled on a pair of khaki shorts and a clean tie-dye T-shirt. When I had begun my studies at the university, I had taken pride in uncovering my Germanic roots. Bizarre Kafka. The ironic prose of Thomas Mann. Rilke's deep and soaring poetry. Nietzsche, the iconoclast. It was from the likes of Hegel that the others had rebelled. *They* had broken free. But Hegel had no rebellion in him. Kant had offered him a bold new view of consciousness by going beyond Hume's mealy objectivism, but Hegel had learned nothing from him. He dropped the ball. *Damn him!* Curse his calcified Teutonic mind!

I punched in Muffy's number. After three rings, someone picked up and said she wasn't in, would I like to leave a message? I didn't really have a message for her, so I hung up. Indecision swamped me as I balanced my options. On one hand, pizza and beer. On the other, Hegel. On this sunny Saturday afternoon, it was no contest. Hegel could wait. I slapped down the hollow stairwell in my flip-flops. The lounge below was strangely deserted. Even the television sat blank and silent, maybe for the first time ever, as if the world had ended. I decided to hoof it over and join the brothers for a little pizza. Maybe even a single beer, as a way of sticking my tongue out at Hegel's rational universe.

In the blinding sunlight I crossed the busy campus thoroughfare and ducked beneath the peeling steel trestle of the elevated. Through the muggy heat I made my way to the city park and the downtown square, where I looked for Pookie's car, but recognized none of the vehicles lining the streets. The pizza joint squatted beneath a brick archwork in the alley below street level. Inside I found crisp air conditioning, but no one I knew. The brothers must have headed out to Papa Louie's in Skokie.

As I reclimbed the brick stairs to the street, I felt something slap my forehead, a wet smack just at the hair line. My first impression was that of a bird. A barn swallow protecting its nest in the eaves above. The blow stunned me for only an instant before I resumed my ascent. Suddenly I was not feeling so well. My knees felt soft and mushy. Emerging at street level, I squinted against the glare for my car. I couldn't remember where I had parked it. Oddly, I couldn't even remember what the car looked like. A woman stepped off the sidewalk to let me pass, her face an expression of horror.

As I crossed the street and entered the park, my gait grew unsteady. Wobbly. I was lighted-headed. Maybe even faint. My vision had grown blurry. All I wanted to do was find my way back to the dark quietude of my own room. Maybe lie down for a bit. I searched for a bench to rest. An elderly couple on the nearest one were gawking at me. Ahead was an empty bench with wrought-iron ends, but I knew I couldn't make it that far. So I lurched down onto the grass to take a breather. As I leaned forward to fish a clean handkerchief out of my back pocket to wipe my brow, I felt something warm and sticky run down my nose and saw red drops splash onto the sidewalk. A trail of splashes led back the way I had come. I raised my handkerchief to my face and brought it down smeared in blood.

What the hell was happening?

My head ached. I felt sick to my stomach. Wearily I lay back on the soft grass, rolled on my side, and threw up.

2

From the sounds and smells, I knew I was in a hospital even before my eyes opened. The same sounds and smells attended my mother as she lay dying. Slowly my vision unblurred, focused, and settled on a rotund figure slumped in the chair next to the bed, sleeping. I knew that person. It was Pookie. I watched Pookie's bald spot rise and fall as he breathed. Jason Puker. Pronounced *"Pooh-ker."* Not *"Puke-er."* Pookie had made that clear as Pledge Master two years ago. Pookie had been a sophomore then. I a freshman. A new pledge. I had hated all that pledging and hazing shit. It was so dehumanizing. Why would an upperclassmen want to treat his pledges so? They spoke of a long tradition. But that made it even worse. Why would anyone make it a tradition to treat another human so? It was the sickness at the core of the fraternity that never ebbed as the years rolled past and each brother learned to dehumanize everyone who did not belong. And even some of those who did.

As my eyelids drooped, I saw Pookie even more vividly. Each hair of his short crewcut that ringed a prematurely balding forehead. The pale ring of a scar. His eyes flaring with power as he handed me six Parodi cigars–six ugly little dry dog turds–and demanded that the pledges smoke them all in the windowless attic room before anyone could come out. I had thrown up that night. But it was not *my* sickness I remembered. It was Pookie's mad eyes. It was an entirely different kind of sickness.

I didn't want to think about it any more, yet I wondered, *why is Pookie in my room?*

3

When I opened my eyes again, the chair was empty. A long yellow shaft of sunlight blazed through the corner of the window and lit the gossamer strands of a tiny spider web. The silver strands were growing, slowly, spiraling out from the center, and I could almost see a tiny black dot of the spider as it instinctively filled a space it had never encountered before. The intricate natural pattern was entirely out of place in the sterile cocoon of the hospital room. Out of place, just as I was out of place. But it gave me joy to watch it grow, around and around, until my eyelids grew so heavy I could no longer keep them up.

4

"Are you awake, Mr. Faehren?"

My eyes fluttered open. I had been dreaming something strange. Something warm and musty and ripe, filled with earthly smells and warm bodies rutting, but not altogether pleasant. Yet I did not want to be awake. Awake I was interred in the beeping and whooshing, the rattling clatter and sterile aromas of the hospital. I did not want to be here. My lids descended as I tried to drift back into my dream.

"I am Doctor Melankov." The name didn't register. I didn't care. Slowly I focused on the tanned face of a middle-aged man with short brown hair and a stubble of salt-and-pepper whiskers. It was a kindly face. The smiling face of a concerned father with features a little too pinched to be handsome. The face was uncomfortably close, the vivid blue eyes studying me. The breath smelled of onions. "How do you feel?"

I considered how I felt. Not so hot, really. I seemed to hover at the center of a throbbing ache, originating above my brow like an internal sun and radiating down through my nerves into every cell and fiber. My throat burned. In the crook of my left arm a sharp pain stabbed like a knife caught in the folds of the gown. I tried to move my arm, but I could not. A wave of nausea rose and swept over me. Or maybe it was hunger. I tipped my head back and forth on the pillow.

The doctor's smile deepened. "Not so good? Well, that's to be expected. You've been through quite a lot, young man." He then proceeded to describe the highlights of the ordeal as if lecturing a cluster of medical students. They had induced a coma. Then they had to remove a portion of the skull above the frontal lobes to relieve the swelling in the brain. It was touch and go for quite a long time. The patient had been unconscious through it all. They kept him going on a ventilator and anaesthetics and drugs and intravenous feeding. He apologized for having to restrain me, but they didn't want me to disturb the temporary plate in the top of my head. Then he paused to assess my comprehension.

But I was barely listening. This had all happened to someone else. *Was happening* to someone else. I was not interested in the grisly details. My tongue was almost too thick to move, and my lips were numb, but I tried to form a single word.

The doctor couldn't make it out. "Anyway," he concluded quickly, still smiling, "now your EEG is looking good. Better than I expected so soon. Your vitals look good. You appear to be out of the woods, young man."

"*Hegel?*" I managed to whisper.

"What? Can you try to say that again. More slowly." Melankov leaned closer. The onions were cloying.

I tried again. "*Hegel . . . exam?*"

"Oh, your exams." The doctor smiled. "Not to worry. That's all come and gone. I'm sure they will let you make them up. The thing now is to get you back on your feet. You can deal with all that when you're feeling better."

I managed two more words, "*Draft . . . board.*"

"Oh, you're worried about being drafted. Into the army? So you're on a 2-S deferment?"

I tried to nod.

The doctor smiled again. "Not with a plate in your head, they're not going to draft you." He glanced up. "Oh, here's Dr. Carver. I'm going to let him have you now." The bed creaked as he rose from its edge. "I'll be back later."

A second doctor, wearing a severe white coat that hurt my eyes, creaked down in his place. "I'm Dr. Carver," he announced brusquely, as if he had too many things to do and too little time to do them. His face was lean and angular, with sharp, deep-set eyes. "I'm your neurosurgeon." He shined a penlight into my eyes. Then he held the silver tube out and said, "Can you follow this without moving your eyes?"

I followed it back and forth.

"Could you see it?"

I nodded.

"Good. Now grip my fingers with both hands and squeeze."

It took me a while to tug my arms free from the sheet. The tube in the left arm tore and pinched. I gripped the man's smooth fingers. Squeezed.

"Good. Now roll your head on your neck. Like this."

I rolled my head a little bit, wincing as a pain shot through my skull.

Dr. Carver made a note. "Can you stick out your tongue?"

I stuck out my tongue.

"Grin and scrunch up your face, like this?"

I did so.

"Good. What's your name?"

I mumbled my name. "*Kahlin . . . Faehren.*" It was unintelligible, but apparently close enough.

"And where do you live?"

I did my best to tell him. And I told him who the President of the United States was, what month it was (though I got that wrong), where I lived, where I was enrolled in school, and what I was studying.

"Good. Where is your father?"

I mouthed the word, "*Dead.*"

Dr. Carver jotted a note. "What'd he die of?"

I tapped my sternum with a finger.

"Heart attack?"

I nodded.

"When was that?"

I shut my eyes. This was too much. I wanted him to go away.

"All right. What about your mother?"

I thought about my mother wasting away in the nursing home in Aurora, unable to recognize me any more. It was all too much right now.

"Good," said Dr. Carver, as he finished scribbling notes onto the chart. "The nurse will get the rest of your history later." Abruptly he stood. "We're going to get you out of here just as soon as we can." I watched him step away, then turn back, glancing through his notes. "You never asked what happened to you," he said.

I thought about it. "*No*," I whispered.

"Why not?"

I didn't have an answer.

Carver scribbled another note and was gone.

5

By afternoon they had me sitting up in bed with a cold metal pan beneath my haunches, while an ancient crone in a striped dress tried to coax me into having a bowel movement. It was impossible. The anesthetics would not ease their grip.

"Please keep trying," pleaded the nurse. Or maybe she was just an orderly, or a volunteer, or some other functionary I didn't really want to know about. "It's been a long time and this is very important," she whined, as if her paycheck depended on my success.

But it was no use. My nether regions were unresponsive, as if they had frozen up during my sleep like an abandoned tractor engine rusting in some field. I felt none of the vital churning and bubbling and contracting and spasming that had always been there before. My body felt like a slab of meat.

And it was more than just my bowels. My mind still slumbered. So did my emotions. My curiosity. My appetite for life. Perhaps it was the anaesthesia. Or the pain killers. But it felt like it went far deeper than that. It felt like my spirit would not wake up.

"Are you still trying?"

I ignored the question and asked instead, "How long?"

"Until you manage to put something in the pan."

"No . . . not that . . . how long has it been?"

"How long have you been here? In the hospital? Didn't they tell you?"

I shook my head.

She circled to consult the chart at the foot of the bed. "Let me see. You were admitted on the fifteenth of September. And this is the eighteenth–"

"Three days? It seems like–"

"Oh, no. It's been over a month. You were admitted in September. Now it's October. A month and three days, you've been here."

It felt like something crucial had been carved out of me. My time. My youth. My heart. "What happened . . . to me?"

She glanced at the chart, then hung it back up. "You'll have to ask the doctor about that."

6

"We . . . ah . . . don't really know." Dr. Melankov shuffled uncomfortably. "A trauma to the forehead. We don't know what caused it. Possibly a stray bullet."

"Bullet?"

"That's what the police are going on. A glancing blow. It's not inconsistent with the wound. We can't rule it out."

"Why?"

"Why would someone be shooting at you? Is that what you're asking?"

I nodded.

Melankov shook his head. "No way of knowing. Probably just bad luck. Anyway, the police will want to talk to you about that."

7

But Detective Dunwitty didn't have any answers either. Only questions. Lots of questions, repeated over and over. In his worn tan sports coat and rumpled brown slacks, the blond, thirtyish Detective sat cross-legged in a chair beside the bed scribbling in his notebook, as he drilled me with humorless questions until I began to feel guilty about some sinister plot I could not quite remember. But there was no plot. And no answer to why I had been struck in the forehead by a stay bullet one month and three days earlier.

When the Detective was gone, I thought about what Dr. Melankov had said. *Just bad luck.* Perhaps. I wondered what Hegel would have thought about such an explanation. *The rational is the real, and the real is the rational.* No room for blind luck. Maybe the philosopher would say that we simply have not discovered the reasons for what happened yet. Ah, but there's the rub. If we are incapable of uncovering the reasons, then from the standpoint of actual experience, how can things be seen to be rational at all. And if this whole thing is not rational, does that mean it is not real?

I squeezed my eyes shut against the dull ache in my head, but I saw Hegel's face superimposed with Pookie's burning eyes. I jerked them open again. *Is all philosophy bullshit?* I wondered. *Maybe I ought to change my major.* When the nurse came in to check on me, I asked her when they were going to discharge me.

"Not until tomorrow at the earliest," she replied. "You doctor wants to keep you another night for observation. And he wants to keep an eye on your EEG."

8

I awoke to a world changed. I was alone in a new hospital room, with the pale glow of dawn hanging outside the window in the east. But I was alive. I pulled myself up on the pillow for a better view. Everything seemed so vivid. The streets were empty. A single stoplight cycled fecklessly between red and green. A terrible serenity pressed down from the low clouds, pervading everything. Nostalgia, perhaps even melancholy, caught in my chest and tickled with each breath. A heavy scent of confusion mingled with the astringent hospital air, coloring it with sadness. Something about the room, something about the drooping branches of the trees outside, something about the silent streets, something at the heart of things, seemed to be undergoing an identity crisis. I was not quite sure who or what it was. I did not know how to relate to it at all.

My mind was clearer now. Soon I would be leaving the hospital. Possibly today. *But where was I bound?* My parents' home had been sold and the proceeds poured into the family trust, administered by Uncle Friedrich. My mom's brother. The trust footed the bill for my tuition and room and board and a little spending money on the side. But the money was draining away to pay for my mother's nursing care. Evaporating. Soon nothing would be left. I had no place to go to rest. To gain back my strength. No place but that solitary room on the reverberating third-floor hallway of the fraternity house. But at least the room and board were paid up for the rest of the semester. Beyond that . . .? I had a little money saved up. Not much. I drew a deep breath. I would just have to do what I had to do to survive.

They wouldn't be drafting me into the army, anyway. "Not with a plate in your head," the doctor had said. That lifted a weight from my soul. But it also severed an overwhelming purpose that had driven me for years: the need to stay in school until I reached twenty-seven, when I would be beyond the clutches of the army. Now . . . adrift . . . everything was different. Now I was free to drop out for awhile. Anytime I pleased.

And that freedom made me giddy.

They fed me a hospital breakfast of scrambled eggs, dry toast, and apple sauce on a rollaway tray. I was hungry. I asked for seconds. Then a nurse and a physical therapist got me on my feet and walked me up and down the corridor a few times. My legs were weak and wobbly, but the therapist and nurse supported me until I got my sea legs. I was still being held for observation, they said. But when I managed to deposit a couple of dried knots into the toilet bowl, that seemed to do the trick. They would begin the discharge process. Doctor Melankov talked to me briefly and warned me to be gentle with my head. A nurse changed the dressing and showed me how to do it myself. Sometime after noon the discharge nurse presented me with a sheaf of papers to sign and left me copies. I had no desire to read them. Then she handed me clean underwear and a sweatshirt, which one of the brothers had brought in from my dresser, and the blood-spattered trousers I had been wearing when I was admitted. I waited in a bit of a daze as I watched the big hand of the clock inch around the dial. I was dozing when a young man arrived with a wheel chair and lowered me down the elevator to the lobby to wait some more.

Like burly defensive linemen, Walter and Brogan and the Chimp surged silently through the glass doors to remove me back to the fraternity. With expressions grim as death and a uncustomary lack of humor, the brothers drove me to the front door and half-carried me up the echoing stairwell. When I was safely inside my room, I watched as they each involuntarily wiped their hands on their pant legs to remove whatever virulent infection they might have picked up. At the hospital. Or from touching the infirm. I smiled. Youth fears infirmity more than all else. I understood. I had not chosen to become this pale invalid, tottering against the desk. I had never asked for this.

9

I hobbled down the hallway to the lavatory, steadying myself against the wall as I went. The door was almost too heavy to pull open, and it whisked me inside as it closed. And there I was in the big mirror above the sinks. Pale. Wasted. Deep sunken eyes. Whiskers on my sallow cheeks. My sweatshirt hung off a skeletal frame. I had lost a lot of weight. I pulled off the thin cotton skull cap they had given me at the hospital, exposing the white bandage pasted to my forehead. A bristle of dark hair was beginning to regrow on my shaved head.

Boomer crashed through the door and went straight to the urinal. "Jesus, you look like hell," he said, inspecting me over his shoulder.

"Hi, Boomer. How's it going?"

"Y'oughta go someplace an' get yourself some R and R. Come back when yer lookin' a little better." He flushed and hurried out still zipping his fly.

I slept for a while and then felt like I needed to tidy up the room. Put my life in order. I put Hegel away. Cleared off the desk. Fluffed up my pillow and leaned against the headboard, staring at the partially open door. Several brothers poked their heads in to inquire how I was feeling. Declining to sit down, they did not stay long. They were careful not to touch anything. But despite everything, I sensed that everything was going to be all right.

Late in the afternoon, Pookie opened the door and stepped inside. As I knew he would. I don't know how I knew, but I did. We had never been close friends. In fact, I probably hadn't spoken a dozen sentences to him over the past three years. But I did know he would be there. With the certainty of an old memory. Just like he had been there in the recovery room at the hospital.

"I'll bring your supper up to you," he said.

"Thanks," I replied, embarrassed by my frailty. "Maybe I'll be able to make it down to the dining room tomorrow."

"Maybe so." He lingered awhile, leaning against the door jamb. Smiling. Watching me. An undeniable force of nature. A round, pale young man with a short crewcut, balding forehead, and piercing eyes. Eyes that seemed to see more than was there. I didn't know what to expect. Finally he nodded, apparently satisfied. He shook his head and said, "I just had no idea that it was going to be *you*."

10

"Spaghetti tonight," Pookie announced an hour later as he punched open the door with his shoulder, balancing a full tray in his hands. "Would you like it there?" He nodded to the bed where I lay.

"Well, maybe I should sit up at the desk."

"I was going to sit there." He motioned for the freshman pledge who stood outside with a second tray to set his on the desk, then dismissed him with a nod. "You'll be fine where you are. Here you go." He handed me my tray.

We ate in silence as I waited for what was coming. As if I *knew* what was coming.

"Mind if I close the door?" Pookie asked, as he rose to close the door. He did not wait for a reply, as I knew he would not. He concentrated on his dinner, and I studied him uneasily as I forked up my spaghetti. Pookie was different. No doubt about that. Oh, he had the same air of entitlement typical of the brothers who had attended expensive prep schools. And he was a social animal and master of diplomacy who had easily gotten himself elected to the governing board of the Associate Student Government. And he was president of the fraternity. Yet, as far as I could see, he had no really close friends. He never seemed to study and engaged in little physical activity. At heart he was a loner, and I wondered why he was befriending me.

But there was something else, too. In truth, Pookie scared me. Something frightful smouldered behind those blazing eyes. Those watchful eyes that saw into the depths. Eyes that never seemed to blink.

The eyes of a predator. After we had eaten in silence for a while, Pookie dabbed his mouth with his napkin, pushed his plate away, and turned those eyes on me. "Do you ever feel like you know things that are about to happen?"

My mouth was full, and I was in no hurry to respond. I chewed slowly, swallowed, and asked at last, "You mean, like I've got it all figured out?"

"No, more like a foreshadowing. More of a *feeling*. More like *remembering* something that hasn't yet taken place. Don't you ever get that feeling?"

"Like a premonition?"

"Something like that."

I was having that feeling then. "Yes," I admitted.

"I call it, 'premembering.'"

"*Pre*membering. That's cute."

"Yeah. And kinda catchy, wouldn't you say?"

I shrugged. *Where was this going?*

Pookie was silent for a long time. Considering. Then he made his decision. "I believe that some of us can actually remember the future," he announced simply. "What do you think of that?"

I thought about it, then shook my head. "There's a big philosophical problem with what you're saying."

"Oh?" He leaned back in my desk chair, amused. "Tell me what the problem is, Mr. Philosopher."

"Well . . . if we can actually *foresee* the future . . . then . . . then the future would be fixed . . . and there would be no free will."

Pookie actually laughed out loud. "Free will is overrated."

"No, really, how can I make decisions about what I'm going to do, if those decisions are already made for me."

"Oh, you still make them," he said. "As you always have made them, and always will make them. But the decisions are always the same."

"But that's not free will!" I protested.

"Call it what you will," Pookie grinned, enjoying the banter. The ice was broken. He was on a roll. "Those are all just words. In truth, the timeline is fixed. Think of it as a roller coaster. No beginning. No end.

You . . . however you want to define yourself . . . you are just along for the ride, thrilling at the ups and downs, screaming at the drops, calculating on the level stretches, making your decisions as you fly along, but in fact the track is already fixed. Set in concrete. Does that idea bother you?"

"Hell yes, it bothers me." The conversation was annoying. Like Hegel, Pookie was presuming to know the unknowable. "What makes you so goddamned certain about all this nonsense?"

He watched me for a while, soft and round as a pale egg in the indirect light from the window. Like one of those little Buddha statues. The ones whose bellies you rub for good luck. But with Pookie, I sensed that the luck he brought might be *bad*.

Suddenly he rocked down his chair, leaned forward, and said quietly, "You look tired. Tomorrow I'll bring up your dinner again and tell you what happened to me." He glanced at the trays and the dirty plates. "I'll send up a pledge to clear out this mess." But he didn't. He probably forgot. Pookie had a lot on his mind.

11

The next morning I managed to hobble down to the dining room for breakfast, then returned to my room for a long nap. It took me the better part of two hours to shave off my whiskers, shower, and change the dressing. After lunch I sat in the sun on the front porch, chatting with the brothers as they came and went. I was feeling better, stronger, though I still tired easily. I returned to my room for another nap.

Pookie brought my dinner again that evening. In anticipation, I was sitting up in the chair to reclaim my proper place at the desk. But it was an empty victory. Pookie didn't seem to even notice. He shut the door behind him, settled onto my bed, tray balanced on his knees, and began eating. We ate in a silence that I found uncomfortable.

"Ten years ago," he said suddenly without preface, "I was riding my bicycle with some friends. Playing a little game we called 'Ditch'em.' I was looking for a place to hide and found this old building down a long dirt driveway on a neighbor's property. I think it was an abandoned garage of some sort." He took a bite of Salisbury steak. "I was eleven years old. Just playing Ditch'em." He ruminated a while, swallowed. "Something happened there. I hit my head. I was circling through the open double doors of that old garage and the wheels slipped out from under my bike on the loose gravel and I fell and hit my head on the old cast iron catch on the center post. I can still picture it. Big. Rusty. Ugly."

I had no idea how to respond.

He looked at me and tapped the pale ring of scar on his forehead. "Like you, I almost died."

I waited while he took another bite, sipped his coffee.

"I reviewed your charts, you know," he continued, turning to see how I'd respond. He didn't say how he'd gotten access to them, and I didn't ask. Pookie had his ways. "Your injury is the same as mine."

"Couldn't be exactly the same."

"Pretty close."

"But . . . your scar doesn't look all that bad," I said.

"Oh, my parents spent a bundle on cosmetic surgery. It seems like I was in and out of the hospital all through middle school." He touched his forehead again. "This was the best they could do."

"I hope mine turns out looking that good."

"Anyway . . . after the accident . . . after the accident something changed. I began to remember things that hadn't happened yet."

I smiled. I knew this was coming. "Premembering," I said.

"Yes." He searched my eyes for something more.

"Like what?" I finally asked. "What did you premember?"

"Lots of stuff." Pookie recounted a number of things. What the teacher was going to ask him to do. Who to avoid on the playground. Who to trust. What would be on the tests. How to get what he wanted. And later, in high school, how to make money by betting on sporting events when he had a hunch who the winner would be. "It was never a hundred per cent," he said, "but it was a hell of a lot more accurate than just flipping a coin."

"So . . ." I said, leaning back, ". . . so what you're saying is . . . is that . . . is that maybe *I* should be premembering things too? Just like you did. And just because our injuries are so similar–"

"No. *No.* Not *just* because our injuries are the same. But because

I've had a clear premonition . . . *for years* . . . a vision . . . a prememory, if you will . . . that I would find someone who has the same ability I have to see the future. Another person. *Here and now* I would find them. At Northwestern. At this fraternity. In my senior year. Someone to work together with me to clarify these fuzzy visions. I *knew* I'd find someone. Someone with the same ability as I have to remember the future. I've been waiting for this to come along. I just never suspected it was going to be *you*."

"I think you've got it wrong," I said. "I'm not the one."

"What makes you so sure?"

"Well . . . for one thing . . . what you're saying is a physical impossibility."

"Why?" he smiled.

"Because nobody can see the future."

"Why not?"

"Because . . . because . . . *it hasn't happened yet*. Because it's the *future*! A person can only remember things that have already happened!"

Pookie cocked his head, amused. "Because the arrow of time flies only one way?"

"Yeah. That's it. Exactly. Because time only goes one way."

"From the past to the future?" he led me on.

"Yeah, from the past to the future."

Pookie smiled, like he *had me* on something. "Who says?"

"Who? Well . . . everybody knows that. It's a one-way street. You *remember* the past. You *plan for* the future. Time only goes one way."

"Physicists have been debating that issue for years," he said simply.

That piqued my curiosity. As he knew it would. "Okay. Suppose you give me the name of one single scientist . . . one *respectable* scientist . . . who says that time can go both directions. A physicist. Someone *I've* heard of."

"Well, let me see, " Pookie said, drawing it out, enjoying himself, "How about . . . say . . . well . . . how about . . . Albert Einstein?"

I was shocked. "You're telling me that Einstein believed time goes in both directions? I never heard of that. How come he never made it public?"

"He did." Pookie rose. "Tomorrow I'll bring you something to read."

He left the trays of dirty dishes when he walked out of my room.

12

The next evening Pookie carried a stack of heavy physics pamphlets and books, bristling with bookmarks, which he plopped down on the bed. A pair of pledges were carrying the supper trays. Pookie received his on the bed and told the pledges, "All right, get on back down to your board jobs."

"Wait a second," I countered. "Could one of you pick up the dirty dishes in about an hour. I'm still a little unsteady on the stairs. I'd appreciate it."

Pookie began eating. Some kind of hearty beef stew with French bread. But I couldn't wait. "You said you had something about Einstein and the flow of time," I prompted.

"Oh, uh huh," Pookie spoke with his mouth full. He reached over and pulled out a small booklet, handing it to me. "Look't this."

It was an account of an 1909 Agreement to Disagree between Walter Ritz and Albert Einstein. I had never heard of Walter Ritz. The account discussed the Maxwell-Lorentz equations, electromagnetic field theory, geometrodynamics, electrodynamic theories, and, indeed, the reversibility of time. Two incomprehensible differential equations climaxed the document. I couldn't understand a word of it. It was worse than Hegel. "So, you're saying, that *this* says, that Einstein believed that time was reversible?"

"Uh huh," Pookie repeated, still chewing. He held up his hand to indicate that it would all be made clear to me when he was done eating. All things in their time.

I poked at my food until he put down his plate. Then he began to patiently explain his understanding of the reversible arrow of time, where physical laws flowed equally easily both ways. He began with Arthur Eddington, the British astronomer who coined the term "one-way arrow of time," talked about the Second Law of Thermodynamics and entropy, touched on Loschmidt's Paradox and Schrodinger's equation, all the while thumping the physics texts like some bible-belt preacher. He mentioned Newton and De Broglie and Werner Heisenberg and Richard Feynman as if he were dropping names at a banquet. He even brought in Hume and the epistemological problem of causality, which, though familiar to me, fluttered meaninglessly past my overwhelmed ears.

"Wait!" I interjected, holding up my hands. "Wait! Wait! I'm not following any of this. Can't you just give it to me in plain English."

Pookie sighed. "Okay. Here's it." He spoke slowly, choosing his words. "The universe is closed. Okay? Einstein showed that. Everything is inside. Nothing outside. There is no *outside* clock to measure the passage of time by. Okay? So all time is inside. It's already laid out. Just like space. Therefore, *all* times are equally real. There is no special 'now'. Okay? There is no distinction between past and present and future."

"And Einstein believed *that*?"

"Absolutely. It comes from his General Theory of Relativity. There's a particular quote . . ." He fumbled through the bookmarks of a fat volume. "Here. I've got it. I've got it. Einstein once wrote a letter to a deceased colleague's family, and in the letter he said . . . let's see . . . *'People like us, who believe in physics, know that the distinction between past, present, and future is only a stubbornly persistent illusion.'*"

None of this was clear to me at all, and I began to doubt that Pookie really understood much of it either. Still, in a way, he had made his point. What he *had* proved, was that even the greatest minds of the century had wrestled with the problem of time's symmetry and were not entirely in agreement. This, standing alone, seemed significant. "Okay," I grumbled. "So. Let's assume you're right. I can't even imagine what it would be like to see time running backwards. I've never seen that. How come?"

Pookie was prepared to shift course. "Evolution," he nodded, knowingly. "Evolution has stuck us in a one-directional reality. Past to present to future."

"What the hell is that supposed to mean?" My voice had risen from frustration. Pookie pretended to have an answer for everything, and it riled me. I wanted to pop his balloon. "It seems to me that remembering *the future* would be far more advantageous . . . from a natural selection standpoint . . . than just remembering the past."

"Of course," Pookie agreed. "But that would invite a paradox, wouldn't it?"

"What paradox?"

"The paradox of free will. Choice. You brought it up the first time we talked about this stuff. Remember? For example, if I were asked to choose between . . . say . . . red or black at the roulette wheel, and I already remembered that I had put my money on red and won, I just might be tempted to choose black this time. Just to see what would happen."

"*You* probably would." I thought about it. "But . . . I think you've just pulled the rug out from under your whole thesis," I said. "The paradox of free will *precludes* premembering the future."

"Not so fast. I think the paradox may prevent us from premembering certain future events, but only the ones over which we might have some effective control. Like choices. Red or black. Soup or salad. Those intimate premonitions . . . those kinds of prememories . . . turn out to be fuzzy at best. Unclear. Inconclusive. If they exist at all. It's nature's way of avoiding the paradox. It's simply impossible for us to premember the immediate details of our own choices. Our own future choices. But *not* of premembering events independent of our ability to change them." He paused. "So, from an evolutionary standpoint, those fuzzy premembrances give no competitive advantage and never developed. Only past remembrances were retained." He watched to see if he had convinced me. "Are you going to finish that French bread," he asked.

"No, go ahead." I handed it to him. After a while I said, "Something's not right."

"I'm listening."

"Okay. Okay. Let's go back to the roulette wheel. And you know that red is going to win–"

"I can't really *know*–"

"Hold it!" I sprang to my feet. "Let me finish. There's something wrong here. If you . . . *sense* . . . that red is going to win . . . but you bet on black anyway . . . just to be perverse . . . just to test the paradox . . . just to see what happens . . . then how could you . . . *premember* . . . how could you premember that you win by playing red, if in fact you play black?"

"Well, for one thing, I don't *know* that I'm going to win or lose by playing red. It's not like remembering something that happened in the past. It's all kind of fuzzy. All I know is that I get a good warm feeling about playing red. Red beckons me. It glows. Not necessarily because I *play* it. Maybe the glow I feel comes from knowing that I am going to play against my own best interest and defy the paradox."

I shook my head and sat down. Pookie was too tricky. Listening to him was like trying to grasp a beam of light he was shining on the palm of my hand. As soon as I closed my fist, it was gone. There was too much philosophy in Pookie's temperament. Too much logic. Too much need for a closed, consistent, comprehensible system. And too damned much drama. "That's crazy."

"Isn't it?" he agreed. "Anyway, whatever I choose is what I've always chosen. If I bet on black, against my own best interests, it's what I always have done . . . and always will do."

"That's crazy," I repeated.

"Yes. But logically consistent, wouldn't you agree? We have to break through the illusion to see the thing in itself." He was sounding more like Hegel all the time.

I tried again. "Tell me how I could premember . . . physically premember . . . something that hasn't happened."

"How can you remember something that *has*? All memory arises from a physical state of your brain. You'll agree with that. But if that physical state is symmetrical in time, if it is symmetrical in a causality that runs both directions, then why shouldn't you have intimations of the future arising from that same physical structure. The brain."

"And all of this is just because of a bump on my head?"

"Yeah. And a bump on mine."

"How did that work? How did that cause . . . all this prememory business?"

He shrugged. "I have no idea."

"Okay. Okay." I held up both hands to stop the confusion. "Let's see if I understand the kernel of what you're saying."

"I'm just saying–"

"Hold it!" I interrupted. "Wait. Let me say it my way. I need to think this through. Now . . . according to Pookie's Universe . . . "

He liked the sound of that and settled back on the bed.

". . . according to Pookie's Universe . . . in order for me to premember something that will happen in the future . . . first of all, I have to be aware of it happening, later, when it actually does happen . . . "

"Right."

". . . and second . . . it has to have a strong impact . . . an emotional impact on me . . . on my life . . ."

"Right."

". . . and, finally, I can't be personally involved in it . . . in a way that my choices would make a difference in the outcome."

"Right."

"Is that it?"

"Pretty much."

"Weird."

"Yeah," Pookie agreed. "Pretty weird."

"I gotta give this some more thought."

13

On the fourth evening, Pookie didn't come. After a while I climbed down the hollow stairwell to the lounge. It was like entering a crowded wake. Two dozen of the brothers huddled somberly together staring at the pale blue light of the television screen, where President Kennedy was educating the nation on the Cuban Missile Crisis. Russian nuclear missiles sat armed and ready on Cuban soil. The United States would consider any missile launch as an attack by the Soviet Union, which would require a full retaliatory response against the Soviet Union. Cuba would be "quarantined" by our navy.

"Blockaded," corrected Deaner. Others grunted agreement. I had never seen them so drained of horseplay and banter. "It means nuclear war," said the Chimp. Pookie sat solemnly in the corner easy chair. The brothers were coming to grips with their own mortality.

Later, Pookie found me in my room and asked, "How do you think this fiasco is going to turn out? Are we going to war?"

"I don't know. This is the first I've heard anything about it. It's a complicated situation. I've got no background."

"It's even better if you don't think too much. What's your gut telling you?"

I drew a deep breath and considered. Something felt right, so I said, "I think it's going to work out. I think they'll settle it."

"No war?"

"No war."

Pookie grinned. "That's what my gut's telling me too."

We discussed what sort of deal might be brokered between the Cold War foes and managed to come pretty damn close to how it all finally worked out. While everyone watched and waited, Pookie was busy. He knew places where he could bet on almost anything and put his money down on the "no war" side. He did have to give away stiff odds, because everyone knew that if Pookie was wrong, and if thermonuclear war did break out, they were going to have a hell of a time collecting on the bet.

14

I began eating dinner with the brothers in the cool, windowless formal dining room in the basement. I found myself involved in more banter and conversation than ever before. With Pookie lavishing so much attention on me, the other brothers wanted to know who I was and what I thought about things. Even the seniors. For three years I had been just a bland fellow, a legacy offered a bid only because my Uncle Friedrich had been president of the chapter twenty years earlier, and he was an alum who contributed annually and generously to the house fund. Oh, I had friends within my pledge class, and I took part in most of the events, had even won the chug-a-lugging contest in my sophomore year, but for the most part, I was just a nameless member of the rank and file. I was doing my time there until I graduated. Suddenly, though, I was no longer a cipher, a legacy to be endured. The notoriety left me uneasy.

I continued to meet with Pookie, usually in my room. Sometimes we went for a walk around campus. We talked about lots of stuff, but mostly the physics of time and what I was able to premember. He tested me on every occasion he could. I think he came to trust my intuition more than his own. Mine was fresh and unsullied. His had worn threadbare over the years. And he was placing bets. He was more involved in the outcome than I was. Occasionally he would share some of the winnings, although he never spoke much about what he was betting on. I had to guess. When the Missile Crisis ended peacefully, Pookie made out reasonably well and offered me a couple of hundred dollars of his winnings. In part, I think, to seal our partnership.

I took the money.

The next day the Associated Press ranked Northwestern's football team number one in the nation. Tommy Myers and Paul Flatley had become an unstoppable passing combination. The following weekend the Wildcats squeaked by Indiana 26-21 in Bloomington. Excitement was building for the showdown with seventh-ranked Wisconsin at Madison a week later. Most of the brothers were going to the game.

"Who's going to win?" Pookie asked me.

I wanted to tell him I didn't know, but I *did* know. And Pookie knew I did. "Wisconsin," I told him.

"Northwestern's favored."

"Doesn't matter."

"How sure are you?"

I thought about it. "I get a real bad feeling. I see passes being completed in the corner of our end zone right below me and a real dark mood settling over the NU fans. A lot of groaning. An ugly mood. The way it feels, the game's not even going to be close."

"You're seeing all this? You're there, at the game?"

"I guess," I sighed.

"And you feel this pretty clearly? Pretty strongly?"

I couldn't deny it. I nodded.

He considered. "Are you planning on going?"

"Oh . . . I hadn't really thought much about it. I'm not fully recovered. I don't know if I'm strong enough. And with the bandage–"

"Let's go," he proposed. "I'll drive. You'll be fine. Trust me. You'll be fine."

15

In my new stocking cap I was appraising my appearance in the bathroom mirror, when Walter shouted up the stairwell that there was a telephone call for me. It was Pookie. "I'll pick you up in ten minutes. Wait for me on Sheridan Road. I've got a surprise for you."

As I stood waiting on the breezy sidewalk, a shiny new maroon-and-white Buick Electra convertible, with the top up and four square portholes high on the side fenders, glided to the curb. Pookie sat at the wheel. He wore a heavy navy pea coat and a black watch cap and looked more like a sailor than a scholar. I slid onto the leather seat and gaped at him stationed in command.

"Y'like the car?" he smiled. "My parents gave it to me as a kind of advance graduation present."

"It's a hell of a surprise," I told him.

"That's not the surprise I was talking about," he corrected. Then, as I watched, he pulled the cap from his head and grinned at me. His head was as bald as a billiard ball, making him look more like that fat little Buddha than ever. "Shaved my head," he declared, beaming wider. "In solidarity. We're brothers, right? We can grow our hair back together."

The gesture moved me. I'll admit that. But it also made me uncomfortable. *What kind of "blood brothers" deal was this turning into? And what would I end up owing him?* But I just smiled and shook my head and stared out the windshield as he accelerated into the flow of traffic to begin the three-hour journey to Madison.

Along the way Pookie did most of the talking. Amid great voids of silence, he talked about his life before the university. He had a girl friend in high school who he had left behind with all the other trappings of suburban Cleveland, harboring no regrets about having moved on. At least that's what he said. But I detected a note of nostalgia in his stories. And possibly an undercurrent of pure fiction. Maybe it was the way he kept glancing over to gauge my reaction. I was flattered that he cared about my opinion. Or it could just be that Pookie had a hard time distinguishing between what he wanted to remember and what had actually taken place. Pookie's narrative was as complex as his fevered imagination. He never asked about me.

It was a perfect autumn afternoon for football. Crisp, clear, sunny. Camp Randall Stadium was just as I had imagined. The marching bands. The stadium overflowing. The pom-pom girls leading our army of white-clad soldiers across the green field. Wisconsin storming out in red. The brothers had bought a block of tickets, and we watched it all from high above the Northwestern end zone. The first half was an ordeal of mistakes and miscues and our inability to punch the ball into the end zone, but we were down only ten points at halftime. Two touchdowns and we would be in the lead. The brothers hollered their lungs out for the Wildcats to open it up. Throw the bomb. Myers to Flatly. Stop pussy-footing around. Trounce the bastards! But Wisconsin scored on its first drive of the second half, when our defensive back missed an easy tackle on the Wisconsin receiver. Then came the pass I had envisioned right below us in the corner of our end zone. The brothers were groaning. The dark cloud settling over us. Wisconsin beat Northwestern 37-6 that day. It was not even close.

When it was over, Pookie handed me five crisp one hundred dollar bills. He had made thousands, he assured me. But on the drive back, after we had fought through the teeming crowd and city traffic, after the November sun had set, he grew sullen. The winnings should have elated him, but it was as if he were let down after the whole affair. And something deeper was troubling him. When I asked, all he could say was, "The darkness."

I thought he was talking about the early sunset, or the oncoming headlights in his eyes. "I can drive, if you want me to," I told him. "My night vision's good,"

But that was not the darkness he was talking about.

I did not press him. For a long time we rode on in silence in that shining new Buick with the leather seats and the smell of new car and money surrounding us. It began to drizzle. Just a heavy mist. But the slap-slap of the wipers and the hiss of the tires on wet pavement and the growl of that big engine were hypnotic. Somewhere near the state line he spoke, as if talking to himself. "I think I'm losing it." He shook his head. "At first I thought it was the Missile Crisis. I thought it meant nuclear war. And then I thought the football game was obscuring things. Because I was so heavily involved in betting."

I waited. When he did not continue, I asked, "What does it feel like?"

"I get no feeling at all. About what's going to happen. Down the road." Pookie drew a deep breath. "It's just a black . . . *thing* . . . in front of me. A shroud. Not a shroud. Something brittle I need to break through." He thought about it a while. "Like an empty mirror."

I said nothing, just counted the windshield wiper beats as they slapped away the rain.

After a while he added, "And I think I know how to break through it."

Again I waited, counting another forty beats before asking, "What are you going to do?"

"Ayahuasca."

The word meant nothing to me. When he didn't go on, I asked, "What's that?"

"You've never heard of Ayahuasca?"

"No."

"It's a drug. I guess you'd call it a drug. Really, it's an interactive combination of plants. An infusion derived from the caapi vine and the leaves of certain tropical plants. A brew. Because of their complementary properties, the mixture works to produce visions. The natives in the Amazon rainforest use it to clarify their minds. They've been doing it for centuries. Given the multitude of species in the jungle, you really have to wonder how the natives came up with the idea to combine these two plants. I read up on it at the library."

"How did you hear about it?"

"Bill Kurtz. It was something he heard in his anthro class. It sounded pretty cool to him, so he thought I might be interested. His Professor . . . Dalton, I think it was . . . only mentioned it once, but said one of his teaching assistants knew all about it."

"Ah," I said. "And you looked up the TA."

"Yeah," Pookie smiled. It came across as a bitter grimace in the dashboard's glow. "He's a fellow named Raul. I dropped by his office and talked to him. Speaks good English. He's kind of a strange little guy, but he actually went down there and took some himself, though he doesn't go bragging about it. The thing is, before he'd give me any details, I had to promise I wouldn't tell anybody else about it." Pookie looked at me. "Now I'm going to have to ask you to promise the same thing."

"Sure," I said.

"I mean it." Pookie was serious. "You swear?"

"Sure," I repeated. "I swear."

Satisfied, Pookie told me Raul's story, as the oncoming headlights strobed intermittently over his bald Buddha head. Raul was a graduate exchange student from Equador. Pookie described him as slender and dark-skinned and always upbeat. Always smiling. He had gone into the Amazon jungle and found a shaman who was willing to prepare the concoction and administer it and guide him. He took it many times. It changed his life. It permitted him to break through an impasse that was hindering the progress of his spirit. To break through his own dark cloud. His own empty mirror. "That's what he told me, anyway. Gave me some very concrete information about how I can do it myself. But I had to promise not to use his name. He didn't want to get involved, in case something goes wrong."

That caught my attention. "What could go wrong?"

"Oh, I don't know. A lot of things, I suppose. I have to fly down to Brazil. Cross the river. Locate the shaman. Get him to agree to take me on. A lot of things." He paused, then brightened. "But if this works . . . if this *works* . . . I'll be able to sense the future again. See it more clearly than either of us has ever seen it before. Every nuance. Every detail."

I too saw the shadow of darkness Pookie was talking about. But I think I knew it meant something else. I think deep inside, Pookie knew it too. I held my tongue.

16

Pookie made his arrangements and asked me to drive him to the airport. My battered old Ford was a tin-can rattletrap compared to his slick new Buick, but Pookie didn't seem to mind as I drove him west to O'Hare airport. He was mostly silent, his mind on things far away. When we finally stood beside the white curb at the departure entrance, he said, "Well, my friend, I'll call you to let you know when my return flight is coming back. You can pick me up, can't you?"

"Sure," I said.

He gripped me in a bear hug, which was not something fraternity brothers did in those days. "You know," he said, pulling back, his eyes moist, "you're my only real friend, Kahlin." He released me and grabbed up his small bag. "Well . . . take care. It's been a great run. And wish me luck."

And I let him walk through those terminal doors without saying a word, though I knew he would not be coming back. Not ever. I think Pookie knew it too. It was my choice to remain silent. And his. We ride the roller coaster of free will, as Pookie says, but the tracks are fixed. We will always make the same choices. But it is that moment I remember so vividly. With so much guilt and an ache in my chest. That moment when I remained silent and stood watching him disappear into the terminal.

17

Pookie did not return for the spring semester. My fears were confirmed. I knew he would never be coming back. I helped carry his things out of his room and place them in temporary storage in the basement. The world had already begun to move on.

An investigator showed up instead, a scrawny old fellow in a brown herringbone suit, with a graying moustache and a nervous tick beneath his right eye, obviously retired from a long career in law enforcement. He asked for me, and when we were seated on the cold metal chairs in the pale morning sunlight outside the front door of the fraternity house, he told me his name was Jones. He had been hired by Stuart's parents.

"Stuart?" I asked.

"Stuart Puker," he replied.

Pookie. "I thought his first name was Jason."

"That's his middle name. Stuart's his first. Stuart Jason Puker."

"What did his friends call him then?"

"I have no idea," Jones said patiently. "His parents call him Stuart. Okay?"

I nodded.

"I understand you were one of the last persons to see him."

I told him that we were friends and that I had dropped him off at the airport. I gave him the date and the time and the terminal. Then I

answered a lot of silly questions that had nothing to do with what I knew
had happened. I volunteered nothing about Raul or Ayahuasca or Brazil,
as I had promised Pookie I would not. Nor the "prememory" craziness
that Jones would not have believed anyway.

Jones returned two more times in the following weeks. I learned
more from him than he did from me. He turned out to be a pretty good
sleuth, tracing Pookie's flight to Rio de Janeiro and then a regional flight
to the City of Manaus at the confluence of the Negro and the Solimoes
Rivers in the heart of the Amazon rain forest. He even found a record of
Pookie's stay at a hotel at the port on the Negro River. There the trail
ended. I had little to add or confirm. I believe Pookie must have taken
a boat across the vast, wide, slowly-flowing brown waters to enter the
jungle on the other side in search of a shaman to guide him in the use of
Ayahuasca. But I don't know that. And I did not share my speculations.

In the meantime, I re-enrolled in school and made up the missed
tests. I met the woman who would become my wife. I knew from the
first that she was the right one for me. Not exactly what you'd call love
at first sight, but I *knew* she was the one. My mother died that summer,
and after months of paying final bills and settling the account, what little
was left in the trust fund was distributed to me. But I no longer needed
the money. I had learned to play the stock market.

I think about Pookie sometimes. His blazing eyes. But now I know
they were blazing not with ferocity, as I had imagined. No, they were
frightened eyes. I know that now. Eyes that saw the black cloud of
nothingness closing in, a sight no man should have to see.

My own dark cloud still lies far away on the horizon. I try not to
think about the future.

Hacienda

1

There was something *wrong* about that old hacienda. From the gravelly shore of Lake Chapala, beyond a rusting hog-wire fence, I could just make out the main house brooding in the afternoon sun at the back of the big lot. Mango and banana and lemon trees and clinging bougainvillea and jacaranda and weeds blocked a clear view of the veranda from the water.

Access was through a wrought iron gate on the cobblestone street on the other side. Passing through that creaking gate was like entering a shadowy jungle of forgotten opulence and hope. Someone no longer remembered had built the single-story dwelling with its Spanish terra cotta roof and all the rooms opening onto a broad veranda of red tiles that faced the lake. But now the floor tiles were dull and worn. Window panes were cracked. Screens were torn. Something broken and dark and sinister lurked beneath the cracking plaster and crumbling mortar that bound together those ancient adobe blocks.

When we took possession (or maybe the hacienda took possession of us), we thought we could bring it all back to its glory days. Exorcize the brooding *espiritus*. But that all came later. In the beginning, we lived across the cobbled street from that wide, prison-like gate and had no idea what lay behind it.

2

Ours was not lake-front property. Charlize and I had purchased, sight unseen, a two-story adobe and brick house on Calle Independencia in Ajijic, Jalisco, Mexico. Charlize was my wife. The purchase was on impulse. We had each received college diplomas and were biding our time in Berkeley with part-time jobs before committing ourselves to careers, when our next door neighbor leaned out of the upstairs window and asked if we wanted to go in with them on buying a house in Mexico. A friend of his was selling it. It was cheap, he said. Our share, two-thousand dollars. One thousand down, and five hundred a year for two years.

It took us a while to get our minds around the concept, but we decided we did want to go in with them. We wanted to buy a house in Mexico. Hell yes, we did!

We arrived in Ajijic on a January evening of our fifth day of hard driving, most of it through a strange new world. A wheel bearing in our overloaded trailer had failed as we climbed the mountainous highway from Tuxpan to Tepic. That had cost us half a day. And Charlize was sick with diarrhea and vomiting when we finally located the house and pulled our rig up tight against the adobe wall on the street. The structure sat empty and overgrown in the gloaming like a forgotten archeological ruin.

Pancho, our three-month-old German Shepard puppy, woke up from his long torpor, shook himself on the cobblestones, and began sniffing around his new yard. Neither the running water nor the electricity was functioning. By flashlight I found a bare mattress on the floor of the upstairs bedroom while Charlize found the toilet. It was a dark hour.

On the stained mattress upstairs we spent a restless night beneath a sweaty sleeping bag. In the morning light I got my first view of our new home. While Charlize slept, I inspected it inside and out. The bedroom ceiling was covered with woven petate mats. The walls were exposed beige brick. The floor tiles were strewn with brittle dead carcasses, mostly cockroaches, but a couple of tiny amber scorpions too. A doorway opened out onto a small, red-tiled upstairs patio, where a concrete water tank perched at the corner of a low masonry wall. Next to the tank was an unfinished room with an unglazed window. In the sunlight of a new day, it all felt quaint and cozy.

A steep, naked-brick staircase with no banister descended into a small livingroom with plastered walls painted a brilliant white. An arched brick fireplace was inset into the front wall. Overhead were shallow arches of smooth red brick. Large red tiles covered the floor. Through a broad white plaster arch was a sun-bright kitchen with its red tile counters, a hand-poured concrete sink, a small electric stove, a refrigerator with its door propped open, and an empty rack for a bottle of purified drinking water. The final quadrant was occupied by a large bathroom with a petate mat stapled onto a wooden frame for a door, a bare concrete tub, and a toilet. We had already filled the toilet, but without water, could not flush it.

Pancho had pushed open the flimsy front door and was scratching his belly with a hind leg on the brick pathway. I stepped outside and patted him on the head.

It appeared as though the brick upper story and patio had recently been grafted atop the two-foot-thick adobe walls of a more ancient structure. My degree had been in architectural engineering, so I couldn't help examining the construction with a technical eye. Steel I-beams had been notched onto the old adobe walls, and arches of brick between the beams now formed the ceiling of the lower story and the floor of the upstairs bedroom and patio. But the steel beams were apparently not tied together. I found no trace of a perimeter band of steel or reinforced concrete to keep the beams from spreading. Adobe is nothing more than dried mud and straw. In the event the walls spread or crumbled or melted in the rain, the brick ceiling would come crushing down.

I supposed it wouldn't matter much unless an earthquake struck.

I was learning the calculus that earlier gringos had grasped when they first found their way into this peaceable Indian fishing village. They were free to build wherever they liked. Whatever they could afford. At whatever risk they were willing to take. Labor and materials were cheap, and no one bothered much with architectural plans or building codes. And if a Chapala building official or a town policeman made a call, a little *mordida*, or bribe, would take care of it. A few pesos would always set things right. It was the Mexican way.

Our lot was narrow and deep. The windowless south wall of our house covered half the street frontage. The other half was blocked by a high adobe wall with a narrow opening for a rickety wooden gate that led down two steps to the cobblestone street.

The west wall of our house was a common adobe wall with our neighbors' abode on that side. A family of three or four generations subsisted there, including a brood of half-naked infants who were destined to inherit their parents' fate. The men appeared to be farmers by the tools they carried over their shoulders each morning as they marched off to work, but where they might have farmed I had no idea. After they were gone, an old woman in a black shawl, bent and frail, would sweep the dirt floor of the house with a straw broom while a yellow dog followed her around. From our common adobe wall a new brick wall had been constructed on our parcel back to an ancient adobe shed, or casita, with its sagging tar-paper roof and vacant openings for doors and a window. The casita marked the front half of our property as a courtyard. We saw and heard little of those neighbors from behind the thick adobe and brick barriers.

A deteriorating six-foot-high adobe wall on the opposite side completed the enclosure of our courtyard and separated us from our neighbors on the east. Half-way back was an opening in the wall created by an old, hand-dug well, which we shared with them. Having been forewarned, we had brought down a new electric, shallow-well pump to replace the rusting relic propped up on bricks against our side of the wall. Our neighbors continued to draw out their water with a leaking wooden bucket to quench the thirst of their family and their pigs and chickens and roosters and dogs and burros. Their hovel of adobe and plywood and sheets of corrugated tin squatted at the far back corner of their lot.

None of our adjoining neighbors spoke a word of English.

The courtyard lawn was overgrown and the surrounding garden beds unweeded. The back half of the parcel was a wilderness of waist-high grass and weeds enclosed by a rusting hog-wire fence. It stretched another hundred feet or so to a stone wall as it climbed the slope away from the lake.

By the time I returned, Charlize had made her way down the steep brick staircase to the livingroom and was slumped in a sagging pigskin equipali chair wrapped in a wool serape. Her freckled complexion was wan and puffy and her usually bright waist-long red hair hung dull and clumped and matted against her neck.

"How're you feeling?" I asked.

"I think I'm going to live. Cramps are gone. Hoping the worst is over." After a pause, she added, "The toilet's full."

"I know. I need to get the electricity going and the pump installed."

I was studying the arched-brick ceiling.

"Beautiful, isn't it?" she said.

"What is?"

"The bricks. The arches. They're beautiful."

I grunted and told her about my structural misgivings. I concluded, "If those steel beams were to separate . . . say, in an earthquake . . . we'd have tons of brick crashing down on our heads."

Her mouth had turned sour. *"Please*, Ben, don't do this now."

"Do *what*?"

She looked like she might start crying. "Don't ruin this for me. I can't take it right now. Just get the toilet to flush, okay?"

I commandeered the wooden bucket that rested on the opposite rim of the well and lowered it by its fraying rope, which threaded through an overhead pulley hooked to a wooden beam spanning the gap in the wall. The water was no more than eight feet down. From the back of the next lot, a stocky *campesino* in an sweat-stained, sleeveless gray T-shirt watched me with sullen eyes, but said nothing. I waved to him, but he didn't return my greeting. He just watched as I spilled the water into a galvanized pail I had found in the casita. I carried it inside and poured the water into the tank on the back of the toilet. It flushed. One catastrophe averted. A dozen more to grapple with.

The electricity was no problem at all. At a small office off the main plaza about five blocks away, I wrote down the street address and signed some paperwork I couldn't read. As I was beginning to unload the trailer, a young Mexican showed up at our gate carrying an extension ladder over his shoulder, extended it, and hooked it over the bottom strand of the overhead wires that ran down our street on concrete poles. I watched as he hand-twisted the exposed ends of two wires sprouting from our meter onto the bare bottom strands of the live power lines, one after the other. No tools. No bucket lift. It took all of two minutes. *"Hay luz,"* he grinned at me, as he folded his ladder. *There is electricity.* We were connected.

Installing the new water pump took a little longer. Reading the instructions that came with the pump was the most time-consuming part. I cannibalized the black PVC intake pipe and band clamps from the old pump and connected them to a new footer valve and the new pump.

Electrical feed wires and the underground water line to the house were already in place, so I connected them and started the pump. Water was sucked from the well and spilled into the tank on the wall of the upstairs patio until it overflowed through a spill pipe into the garden. Cold water now ran from the sink faucet and the shower head. The toilet flushed, refilled, and flushed again.

Charlize was dying to take a shower. I found what appeared to be a wood-burning water heater mounted on the outside adobe wall of the bathroom. In the casita I had seen some old newspaper and a cardboard box filled with wooden slats and twigs that had been snapped into foot-long lengths. I lit a small fire and waited anxiously from a distance to see if the contraption would heat the water or blow up. It creaked and banged and popped with increasing violence as the fire crackled. I added scraps of wood until bursts of steam and water spurted from a pipe on top.

"I think your water's hot," I called inside. "Try not to get any of it in your mouth. It's well water."

I kept the fire going, pumped a little more water into the tank, and after she was done enjoyed my own hot shower. There wasn't much pressure, but the flow was good. The cleansing made us both feel a whole lot better. Charlize was cheerful and smiling as she bent into the sunlight brushing her straight red hair with long inside strokes. I loved to watch her brush her hair.

3

Those first days were busy ones as we tried to turn that house into our home. We swept up dead varmints and washed the floors and wiped down the walls and surfaces and began hauling our stuff in from the station wagon and our trailer. I reinforced the front gate with an old board to keep Pancho in the yard. We found the village market, where we bought vegetables, and the supermercado on the plaza for everything else. We lugged home a giant bottle of purified water and installed it in the rack in the kitchen for drinking and cooking.

In the process, we began to meet some of our neighbors who, like us, were expatriates from the United States. *Norteamericanos*, the Mexicans called us. Or *gringos*. In our spectacular hubris we referred to ourselves as "Americans."

Lona, a loud, crusty, irascible old retiree from down the block, insisted that labor was cheap down here and we really needed to support the local economy by hiring some help. Later that day, unannounced, she led a male and female Mexican to our front door and demanded that we interview them while she translated. Lona's Spanish was pitiful, but that didn't faze her.

Ophelia was a small, dark, smiling young woman who needed a little extra money to help her husband, a laborer, make ends meet for the family. She offered to do the housework and the laundry a couple of hours each morning. Towering beside her was a tall, gaunt, middle-aged man in huaraches, khaki trousers, and a long-sleeved white shirt. His jaw was square and bristled with graying stubble. His body seemed bent unnaturally to his right as he clutched a straw sombrero nervously in his gnarled fingers. Manuel, Lona explained, spent much of his time tending his goats in the hills above town. He had injured his back in an auto accident, but would still be able to work for us as a part-time gardener three days a week. They would both be happy to work for very little.

We ended up hiring them both.

None of this was what I had expected. For one thing, I had never been outside the United States, and rural Mexico in those days was about as foreign as foreign gets. I didn't speak a word of Spanish. Couldn't even count to ten. But word by word, phrase by phrase, I began to learn. Gentle, shy Manuel became a patient teacher and a companion as he raked leaves beneath the spreading mango, mowed the grass with an old push mower he borrowed from Lona, weeded the garden and flower beds on his knees along the brick pathway and bare adobe walls, and stood watering everything from an old coil of hose we found by the pump. Sometimes we worked together at odd jobs around the yard, mended fences, or planted a vegetable garden in the back of the lot.

Charlize had taken a little Spanish in high school and adapted more readily. She was soon chatting in Spanish and laughing with Ophelia each morning as the young woman washed dishes and swept and mopped the floor with petroleo-spiked well water to keep the scorpions at bay. On Tuesday each week, Ophelia would carry a bundle of our dirty laundry down to the lake shore where she would wrestle them against the rocks while she gossiped with the other washer-women, then hang them on a clothesline Manuel and I installed in our yard.

Soon the house felt clean and bright and comfortable. The courtyard became a green, manicured garden oasis, like so many others in town that were hidden behind the stark adobe walls that lined the streets like walls of a canyon. The cobbled streets of Ajijic reflected the drab earthen tones of adobe and brick and, in newer construction, reinforced concrete blocks. In contrast, the plastered store fronts near the plaza were brightly painted in broad swaths of reds and yellows, greens and oranges and even blues, often inset with vivid ceramic tiles. Seldom was architectural wood exposed. Lumber was expensive and had to be imported.

Pancho was thriving in his new environment. I had brought a book on German Shepard obedience training and began putting him through his paces each morning. *Sit! Stay! Come! Down! Heel!* He loved the attention and tried hard to please me. Or at least as hard as a puppy's fractured attention would allow. We were beginning to bond. On the streets, however, I still carried his thick leather leash and had to use it often. *"Morde?"* children would whine as they cringed away. *Does he bite?* He frightened many adults too. Though still just a puppy, Pancho was a very *big* puppy, and I learned to reply, *"No. No morde."* He was more likely to lick them to death than bite.

As those first weeks wore into months, I got my hands into a dozen different projects, major and minor. First, we had to keep Pancho in the yard when we left him alone, so I rebuilt the front gate and anchored the frame into the adobe wall with long lag screws and mortar. A two-by-four dropped into place to bar it securely. From the outside, a rope through a hole in the gate allowed the bar to be raised, unless a wooden wedge had been inserted to prevent it. Manuel found the mechanism very clever. *Muy listo.* Then I blocked the openings in the casita with rough wooden shutters and strung hog wire with a gate to close off the back of the parcel. Manuel helped me with the fence.

I also fashioned sturdy new double front doors for the house, with little screened windows in them. Manuel told me where the lumber yard was in Jocotepec, and gave me some other tips, like how to stain the finished doors with old motor oil free from Lupe's garage. I hauled boards and sawed them and glued and screwed them together and sanded them and finished them by rubbing in the motor oil and coating the finished product with polyurethane. Manuel admired the new doors. "*Dos puertas,*" he called them. "*Muy bonitas.*"

I built a dog-house cover for the well pump and an electronic bell ringer to let us know when the water tank was full. I hammered together a low platform for our mattress and we made a canopy out of a sheet and hung it over the bed to keep scorpions from falling on us from the petate ceiling. Working with Manuel, I dug and turned the soil and planted and irrigated a small vegetable garden behind the casita.

We settled into the rhythm of Mexico, accepting routines that seemed so alien at first. Like shaking out your clothes and knocking your shoes against the floor before putting them on, lest there be scorpions. Hauling in the big glass bottles of drinking water and returning the empties to the supermercado. Running the pump whenever the water tank ran dry. Kindling a wood fire for a hot shower. Buying a burro-load of firewood whenever the old Indian brought his heavily laden burros down from the hills. Having no telephone or television for distraction. Little things that seemed so strange and onerous in the beginning grew quaint and charming as the time wore by.

4

Ajijic was a popular place for Americans to retire, so there was plenty of English spoken around us. Many of the retirees were ex-military, whose pensions went a lot further in Mexico. But there were others, surviving on social security or living on the interest of a small inheritance or a lifetime of saving, who found they could live more comfortably down there. And then there were the ostentatiously wealthy, who lived a luxuriant and secluded lifestyle behind locked gates on the lake front or in the hills above, and the merely ostensibly wealthy, like the Brinkerhoffs.

Mitchell and Vivian Brinkerhoff had purchased a small rancho just outside Ajijic. They entertained a lot and invited us to one of their parties almost as soon as they heard through the grapevine that we had arrived. Mitch was overweight and pallid and flaccid and loved to drink martinis in the afternoon and tell stories about himself. Vivian was a mousy little thing with died brown-red hair who never seemed to get drunk or lose control, no matter how much she drank. She kept Mitch on a tight rein. They loved to collect healthy young men and women around them for an audience, and I guess that's why we were there. Especially Charlize, who would light up the old man's eyes just by walking into the room. Vivian accepted it. She'd seen it before, and nothing could possibly come of it. And the jealousy it sparked made *her* feel younger too.

The Brinkerhoffs had a stable full of horses on their ranch. Thoroughbreds mostly. Mitch soon invited Charlize to help exercise the horses whenever she felt like riding them along the lake shore or into the hills. Charlize was ecstatic. She took him up immediately and often. Occasionally I would ride with her, but less frequently as time passed. Mostly she rode alone or with her new friend Anita, a blonde California-born girl who had grown up in San Miguel de Allende with her expatriate parents and then, to their dismay, had married Javier, a bright and bookish young Mexican from Ajijic.

Charlize' favorite was a thoroughbred mare named Lucera. Lucera was lean and muscular, but a little too high-strung for my taste. When I rode, I would pick Lazaro for my mount. Lazaro was a gelding with the same thoroughbred color and markings as Lucera, including the white star on the forehead that gave the mare her name. But there the similarity ended. Lazaro was plump and lazy and easily led. The only time he showed any enthusiasm was when we would turn back toward the barn, where fresh oats and hay awaited. But that was fine, since I was an inexperienced rider. In fact, most of my riding had been on Lazaro, alongside Charlize. Sometimes we took longer rides, like when the moon was full and a small mixed group of gringos and Mexicans rode into the hills with bottles of tequila for a Lunada. We always let the horses find their own way back on the dark, narrow path down the ravine, while we riders laughed and sang and swayed drunkenly in the saddles.

Plenty of other Americans passed through Ajijic too, or stayed for a while before moving on. Younger ones, far from retirement, who still needed to earn their daily bread, by hook or by crook. Some, like Anita, had been brought there by their parents and attended Mexican schools, where they easily picked up fluent Spanish. But there were others, like us, who just wanted the adventure of trying something new as we pissed away our meager savings. We gravitated to Bob and Mary Goldberg. They were a couple of years older than we, but we hit it off with them from the first. They had opened an ice cream parlor just off the plaza they called "Helados Alohas." We spent many pleasant hours there at the metal tables on the open deck reading the English newspaper from Mexico City and bantering or gossiping or discussing world events or philosophy with them or else playing chess with our other young friends and a few English-speaking locals.

The most precious thing we had there was time. And the most mysterious. Mexican time. Time to explore. Time to learn. Time to agonize. Time to reflect and create. Time to make love. Quiet time. Busy time. Idle time. Six months passed before I really began to feel relaxed. Relaxed like I hadn't felt in all my adult life, buffeted as it had been by formal education and part-time jobs. We fell into a rhythm. Into a groove. Charlize developed her routines, and I mine. The days went by and our lives grew deceptively tranquil.

5

Charlize had a thing about animals. All kinds of animals. When I first met her, she had a yappy little poodle mix named Bugsy, who always seemed to be underfoot. Sometime before we were married, Bugsy disappeared. Maybe he ran away or maybe he was dog-napped for a pet or for medical research at the university labs. We never knew. Charlize, of course, was heartbroken and wanted another dog.

I held out, but ultimately realized that domestic tranquility required compromise. Finally I gave in, but only on the condition that I could participate in the selection and training of the animal so we would end up with an intelligent and well-trained companion dog. A German Shepard was my suggestion, and I helped choose a puppy from a breeder in northern California. By then we had committed to the house in Ajijic, so we named him "Pancho."

And there were the cats. A black-and-white stray gave birth to five kittens in the casita shortly after we arrived. Charlize insisted on keeping them all. Each morning she would walk down to the lake, or send me if she was too busy, to buy a bowl of *charales*, sardine-sized little whitefish, from the fishermen as they were hanging out their nets to dry. A peso's worth of *charales* fed them all for a day. Eight cents. But other strays showed up and the kittens had kittens of their own, so by the end of summer we had nineteen cats in the yard and a five-peso-a-day cat food bill. One morning the Mama cat was missing. I found her floating in the well. Then a plague of some sort swept through the rest of the cats and pared them down to three. We buried the dead cats in a mass grave in the back of the lot, alternating corpses and soil like layers of a cake. Charlize was in tears.

So I shouldn't have been surprised when Charlize came home one afternoon in the early fall and informed me, "I'm going to buy Lucera." The Brinkerhoffs, she explained, were moving back to Oklahoma and were planning to sell off their horses. All of them.

"When?" was my knee-jerk question.

"Right away."

"How much?"

"Only two hundred dollars."

"American?"

"Yes, American," she replied frostily, as if she had been anticipating my obsession with detail. She saw it as obstructionism. "But it doesn't matter. I'll use the money my parents gave me for graduation."

That money had already been spent or commingled with our dwindling investments, but I saw she was in no mood to argue the point. "Where would you keep a horse?"

"In the back of our lot. We have plenty of room we're not using back there."

Some things present themselves as inevitable. Irrefutable. You know you are powerless to oppose them. Like aging and death, although neither of us yet paid much attention to those. At least she didn't propose to buy Lazaro too. I let out a deep sigh and resigned myself to adding a horse to the family. Who was I to say no?

With Manuel's advice and assistance, I constructed a rough *caballeriza*, or horse shed, on the back of the lot. It was a shoddy, makeshift affair, cobbled together from wood and corrugated tin and tar paper, but it did the job. I attached a lean-to, enclosed by a smelly canvas tarp, to hold a couple of bales of hay and the tack. And sometimes, in the evening mostly, with the shadows lengthening and the cicadas suddenly still, I would stand out there beside Lucera with an arm across her warm, sleek neck, without speaking, just she and I, and feel entirely at peace with the world.

6

In mid-November Ajijic celebrates its biggest fiesta honoring San Andres, its patron saint. For two weeks the streets were swept and booths built on the plaza and a scaffold-like *castilla*, a huge fireworks display, was erected in front of the church. Friends of ours from Berkeley happened to fly down to visit us at the same time. The night of the big fiesta we met local friends on the plaza and drank tequila and bottles of beer and smoked some marijuana someone had scored from the drummer in a Mexican band. Some American students visiting from Los Angeles had managed to bring along a tank of nitrous oxide. In their apartment we would turn the valve on the big tank and suck in the laughing gas until everything became unreal and loud and bright and skyrockets exploded in the night sky and bells rang and mariachi bands pumped out Jaliscan rhythms and everyone danced and swayed and fell down and got back up again and pretty soon I was throwing up in the bathroom of someone's apartment and then going back outside again to sing and wave my arms and shout out my youth.

Charlize and I both felt awful the next day as we drove our friends back to the Guadalajara airport. We had been in Mexico almost a year and had gotten into the habit of drinking too much, which we had sworn we would never do. Maybe not every day like so many of the older alcoholic retirees, but we would binge hard when we did. We needed a break. We needed a change.

As our first-year anniversary in Mexico approached, Charlize and I decided to take a month-long tour of the southern and eastern regions of the country. It was to be a sort of celebration. A time for reflection and evaluation. Our long sojourn in Mexico had brought with it habits and patterns and attitudes and a subtle stagnancy that needed to be aired out. Allowed to breathe. Shaken up. The deck needed to be reshuffled. We agreed that it would be good for us to get away by ourselves and reconnect. Ophelia would look after the house and Manuel would tend the garden while we were away. Anita agreed to ride and feed Lucera.

We visited the *Museo Nacional de Antropología* in Mexico City and the ruins of Teotihuacan, then spent several days at the Mayan jungle ruins of Palenque. I liked Palenque because the tourists were so few and Pancho was free to explore unleashed. From there we drove to Merida in the Yucatan, where we rented a hotel room on the unexpectedly European central plaza, and explored the ruins of Chichen Itza and Uzmal and a dozen other archeological sites. One night we slept on the white sand beach below the ruins of Tulum. Then we dropped down through the Olmec sites of the Isthmus of Tehauntepek and spent a week visiting the remote Indian village of San Cristobal de las Casas and Monte Alban outside Oaxaca.

Charlize and I rediscovered the intimacy that seemed to have been evaporating in Ajijic. "I'm like a kite," Charlize said to me one night as we were snuggled in a lumpy motel bed on the outskirts of Oaxaca. "Always blowing with the wind." She smiled at me. "And you are my anchor. You keep me from flying away. We're bound together."

7

That whole first year we had paid little attention to the empty, brooding hacienda locked behind the iron gate across the cobbled street. Except for a couple of initial exploratory trespasses, when we explored the grounds out of curiosity. But one day I noticed a scratched and faded white ford van parked behind the gate of the lake-front lot. A day or two later, as Charlize and I were closing our front gate on our way to the post office, the beat-up old van rattled down the cobblestones and pulled up in front of us. A thin young man jumped out of the driver's side and walked over to open the iron gate. He appeared nervous, with wispy blonde hair and a scraggly attempt at a Fu Manchu moustache draping down from his pale lips. Pancho was straining on the leash to make a new friend, but I approached the fellow cautiously. "Hi," I said. "We're your neighbors. Ben and Charlize. And this is Pancho."

"Howdy," he replied, turning to greet us with a broad smile.

Obviously not a dog person, he was doing his best to ignore, yet stay clear of Pancho. "My name's Ken. And that's Betsy in the van. Ken and Betsy . . . Thornton."

Charlize offered him her hand. "Nice to meet you." I thought for a moment he was going to kiss it. But he took it gently and nodded with a sort of bow.

"I met Betsy in the market yesterday," Charlize said. "But I thought she said her name was *Thorn*. I remember because I have a cousin named 'Rose' who married a man named 'Thorn' and I always thought it was funny, you know, Rose and Thorn–"

"No, *Thornton*. Ken and Betsy *Thornton*." Ken glared at Betsy through the windshield. "Thorn-*ton*," he emphasized to her. I thought at first we might be witnessing some sort of lovers' spat. Only they felt more like co-conspirators than lovers.

Ken pulled the van through the open gate and we followed it inside. While Charlize was helping Betsy carry bags of groceries through a brick arch into the courtyard, I hooked Pancho's leash on the gate and approached Ken. He was standing by the van's open door, lighting a cigarette. "Say, Ken, I was wondering if you've got some space where we could park our trailer over here. We've got no place to put it. The street's so narrow out there. I don't like the way our house juts out into it. More than any other house on the block."

He calculated for a moment, then smiled broadly. My impression was that of a slick used-car salesman about to make us a special deal we couldn't refuse. "Sure, bring it on over. I don't see why you couldn't stick it over there behind that wall, if you don't mind the weeds."

"Hey, that's great. Thanks. And we'd be happy to give you a little rent for the space."

He waved the idea away. "No need. I'm sure we'll figure out some other way to return the favor. We're neighbors, right?"

"Right." I searched for something more to say. "So . . . do you own this place?"

"No. We're renting it. Our friend Bobby found it for us. He's a Mexican national. Knows lots of people here and how to get things done."

"How long have you been living down here?"

I saw a flicker in his eyes that told me he didn't like being interrogated. Especially about personal matters. "Not long," was all he said.

It took me about ten minutes to hook up the trailer, pull it through the wide gate, and back it carefully into the weedy corner by the wall. No one was around to help me. Not even Charlize. But I managed. I wheeled the station wagon back onto the street and parked it. Pancho I left in our yard, where he whined softly to himself at the unfairness of it all, as dogs do.

I found my way back through the iron gate and closed it behind me. Through the brick archway Charlize and Ken and Betsy were seated in broken and torn equipali chairs on the dirty tiles of the veranda, chatting and laughing and passing a bowl of tortilla chips. I joined them without adding much to the conversation.

The front wall of the old house and the brick wing walls on both sides defined the inner courtyard, which had obviously once been well planted and tended. Banana trees splayed their broad leaves beside the brick walls. Once the view had been open all the way to the lake. Now it was overgrown and secluded. Weeds and grass and vines were left untended. The windows of the house were cracked and hadn't been washed for a long time. Neither Ken nor Betsy seemed to take much pride in the hacienda or the grounds. It felt to me that their stay was more like an overnighter in a grim hotel. Like they were just passing through. Maybe like they had been running away from someplace else far worse.

We didn't stay long. Just long enough for me to confirm my first uneasy intimations about that hacienda. And of Ken and Betsy, for that matter. Something was fundamentally *wrong*.

As we retrieved Pancho and walked toward the plaza, Charlize filled me in on what she had learned while I was parking the trailer. Betsy was the talker. She and Ken had come down from somewhere in the Los Angeles area a month ago. They had relocated quickly with only what they could carry in their van. Their friend Bobby had told them about Ajijic and had arranged for the rental. Bobby was intending to join them soon. Bobby and his girlfriend Sharon. Or maybe she was his wife. They had all been very close back in LA.

As the days went by, we would spend time with Ken and Betsy. On their veranda or in our own front yard. Talking. Drinking tequila or beer.

In truth, I didn't like either one of them very much. There was something peculiar about Betsy. Something immature. Almost childish. She was too high-energy for my taste, as if those blond curls were wound too tightly around her pale head, squeezing her brain. Betsy was a few years younger than either of us. In her mid-twenties, I would guess. It's not that I actually disliked her. It's just that I wasn't overly fond of her. She was slightly built and skinny and had done lots of drugs before settling with Ken in Ajijic. "Heroin," she once boasted, showing what she claimed to be needle tracks on the inside of her arm. Myself, I couldn't make them out. And speed. Betsy had done lots of speed, she said, and I believed her, because it seemed to still be running riot in her system.

Ken I liked even less. Something blatantly amoral and selfish about him put me off. He was a something-for-nothing kind of guy. The center of his own universe. He felt the world owed him a living. A couple of years older than Betsy, he ran the show. No, I didn't like him one bit, even before all the trouble started.

8

With the coming of the New Year things seemed to enter a new phase. Our five-hundred-dollar payment for the house had come due, and I was surprised to see how much of our nest egg we had managed to burn through during that first year. We had never really planned beyond that first year. We were young, with more enthusiasm than wisdom. I supposed all along that we would return to California when our money ran out and resume whatever it was we were destined to do there. Maybe return to Mexico as time and money allowed. Charlize and I hadn't talked about it much.

Charlize had fallen in love with Mexico. Back in California, she was just one more woman in a sea of young women. But in Mexico, she was special. She was a *Norteamericana*. All the young Latino men, with their tawny skin and brazen *machismo*, were drawn to her. And she finally had the horse she had always wanted since she was a child, and the time to ride it. She rode through the streets of Ajijic like a princess. Mexico seduced her completely and she didn't want to think about leaving.

I felt a specialness there too, but not in the same way. Not so deeply. I felt more like Hemingway and the other expatriate artists must have felt in the coffee shops of Paris. I had taken up writing short stories in the mornings while Charlize went out for her rides. I played basketball with my new Mexican friends and chess with our compatriots at Helados Aloha. But I couldn't shake a realization that things were coming to an end. There wouldn't be much left after the mortgage payment.

Neither of us wanted to pack up and go, but we had trouble discussing our options. As the days wore by and money was spent, I knew we had to discuss them. Time, which once seemed so boundless and promising a landscape, had grown constricted. I now felt cramped with the furniture of our daily habits and routines and compressed by a cloying dread. Charlize was the kite, blowing with the breeze, enjoying life without worrying too much about the details. I handled the details. I was the anchor that bound the kite string.

One morning as I sat at the kitchen table and Charlize fried eggs and bacon at the stove, I knew it couldn't wait any longer. "Charl," I said, "we need to talk."

She acted like she hadn't heard me. She turned the eggs and pressed the sizzling bacon with the spatula. Early morning sunlight beamed through the window.

"Charl?"

She lifted out the strips of bacon and laid them out on a paper towel to dry. Her jaw was set.

"We need to talk," I repeated. "Charlize?"

She brought over the loaded serving plate and slammed it down hard enough to break open one of the sloshing eggs. Yoke ran over the rim onto the pig-skin surface of the table. She faced me squarely. "So what do you want to *talk* about, *Benjamin*?"

"Nothing," I started to say, but checked myself. I drew a deep breath. "We're running out of money," I said. "We haven't even made our mortgage payment. This can't go on."

She glared at me. "What are you proposing?"

"We can't stay here."

Her eyes blazed. The muscles in her jaw stood out.

"We have to make plans to go back," I continued. "Maybe we can work for a year, make some more money, and if you want to, come back for another year."

She threw up her hands. "Why do you *always* have to do this, Ben?"

"Do what?"

"*What you're doing!* Ruining *everything*! It was such a beautiful morning. I was watching the sun sparkling in the dew drops on the grass. And you had to bring *this* up again and ruin everything."

"But we have to–"

"*You* go back if you want to. I'm not going. I'm not about to give this up. All *this*. Just to be a substitute teacher in the ghettos of Oakland. Do you have any idea what that was like?"

I shook my head.

"I'm staying here," she pronounced.

"But–"

"I'll figure out a way," she said, closing the dialogue.

So we held off writing the mortgage check. Charlize found a job as a salesperson in the gift shop at the looms. The *telares*. Where the local indigenies wove blankets and serapes for well-heeled tourists to buy in the store. The base pay was a pittance, but commissions were good and tips could be generous. I tried my hand at selling real estate from a small, bleak office near the local posada. It was purely on commission, and few tourists ever stopped in. I never made a sale.

9

One afternoon in late February I climbed the step and tugged on the rope to open our front gate. Nothing happened. The bar clacked, but would not rise. Pancho barked behind the wall. I stepped back down to the cobblestones, my basketball hooked beneath my left arm, and let out a deep sigh. I was tired and sore and wet from sweat and a sudden afternoon thunderstorm, an unexpected orphan of the departed monsoons. Ajijic had just lost an important game to neighboring Jocotepec. It had been a physical struggle on the concrete court behind the church, and I hadn't played well. Any advantage my height should have given me had been neutralized by the bruising play of our opponents. My lip, split by a flying elbow, was swollen and throbbing. I was cold.

And now the front gate was locked from the inside.

"Charlize!" I yelled and clanged the little bell. "Charlize!"

I heard the front door open. "Ben?" Charlize called softly. "Is that you?"

"Of course it's me. Who else would it be? Open the gate."

She pulled out the wedge and lifted the bar. "Quietly," she admonished.

"Why?" I bulled my way into the yard. "What's going on?"

"Oh!" she said, seeing my lip. "What happened to you?"

"S'nothing. I took an elbow. Why did you lock the gate?"

"Hush," she said. "Betsy's inside. Lying down. Ken beat her up last night."

"Ken did? What for?"

She restrained me by the arm as she replaced the wedge to hold the bar. "I think you should stay outside for a little while. Okay? Betsy needs a little peace and quiet."

"How bad is she hurt?"

"I don't know for sure. She has a black eye and her face is swollen. Ken knocked her down and kicked her. But I don't think her nose is broken. I think she'll be all right. I just don't know."

Charlize brought out my sweatshirt and a beer. I swapped the sweatshirt for my wet T-shirt and sat in the afternoon sunlight sipping beer and thinking things over. The basketball fiasco was forgotten. Spousal abuse was new territory for me. I couldn't understand it. From either perspective. I had seen some bruises on Betsy's arm and the side of her neck a while back, but figured it was none of my business. Now it *was* my business, and I was unaccountably angry. The police seemed like a bad idea in a foreign country. I had no idea who else to call for help.

Suddenly the bar on the gate clacked. It clacked again. Then again. *"Betsy! Are you in there?"* It was Ken calling. *"Lona saw you come in here. Betsy!"*

Pancho, no longer a puppy, growled low in his throat. His big ears were locked on the gate as he started to get up. *"Down!"* I rasped. *"Stay!"* Something in my tone must have conveyed my seriousness. He sank back onto the grass.

As I walked to the gate, I drew a deep breath, then exhaled slowly, removed the wedge, and pulled it open. Ken was looking up from the street below and tried to climb inside. But I blocked his way.

"Betsy's in there," he accused me. "I want to see her."

"Betsy doesn't want to see you right now," I told him calmly.

For a moment I think he considered trying to push past me. We sized each other up. He was a scrawny little fucker. But dangerous. I outweighed him by thirty pounds and held the high ground. He noted the bottle in my hand and heard Pancho's low growl from across the lawn. Then he saw my swollen lip, and thought better of it. "She's my wife," he demanded. "I want to see her. I have a *right* to see her."

"Not if she doesn't want to see you."

He glared at me. I saw that he was capable of violence. But I had just warmed up with a rough-and-tumble basketball game, and I was ready. My heart was pumping and I was angry. "This is our property," I told him at last. "And you're not welcome right now." I pushed the gate closed in his face, barred it, and inserted the wedge.

"Tell her I'm sorry," wafted over the adobe wall. "*Please!*" he pleaded. "Tell her it won't happen again."

I never saw Betsy's battered face that day. I walked out back to work off my pent-up anger with the hoe in the vegetable garden. By the time I returned to the house, Betsy was gone.

"She went home," Charlize said.

"Back to Ken?" I asked, astonished.

Charlize nodded. "She's sure he loves her. Down inside. That's what makes him so jealous."

I didn't see much of them after that. Betsy no longer stopped by our house or invited us over to theirs. She would chat with Charlize when they ran into each other at the market, but always with a wary eye out for Ken. Ken didn't want her anywhere near us. Betsy always seemed to have fresh scratches and bruises on her face and arms. The few times I encountered Ken driving his van down the street, he would look the other way. As if he hadn't seen me. I began to understand that he didn't like me any more than I liked him.

10

And then one day Betsy was gone. We never saw her again. The rumor was that she had run off with a young Mexican guitar player from the local band whom she had met just a couple of weeks earlier. I didn't blame her. In fact, I applauded her and hoped things worked out.

For a week or so Ken moped around, haunting the streets in his battered white Ford van and drinking heavily at the hacienda across the street. Bobby and Sharon filled the vacuum by moving into the main house with him. Trying to raise his spirits, I suppose. But it was of no use. That old hacienda had won.

Then Ken too was gone.

Bobby and Sharon moved in permanently. Into the hacienda across the street. Behind the wrought iron gate. Our relationship with them was cordial, but never close. We did spend a little time with them on their veranda. Quiet time. Drinking a beer or *Cuba Libre*. Never really getting drunk. Bobby seemed uncomfortable at our house. Somehow we didn't fit into his vision of who he was and where he was going. He was a *Chicano* renegade. Perhaps we were a little too straight. A little too establishment. A little too *Norteamericano*. I understood.

I liked them both. Sharon was an attractive, well-built woman, taller than Bobby. Like a showgirl. But she was quiet and didn't reveal much about herself. Her scant conversations were directed to Charlize, not me. She claimed to be married to Bobby, but I had my doubts.

Bobby was fluent in Spanish and English from having grown up in Los Angeles in the home of illegal immigrant parents where only Spanish was spoken. He had relatives in Jalisco and had visited an uncle in Ajijic many times over the years. Ken and Bobby had become friends in high school before they both dropped out to engage in private enterprises which were never specified, but which I assumed were illegal. Ken had gotten into serious trouble, again unspecified, and had taken Betsy with him on the run. Bobby set them up in Ajijic. Bobby confirmed that Betsy was living somewhere near Mexico City and that Ken had returned to Los Angeles. Neither was planning to come back.

Time wore on. The weather grew hot and dry and the cicadas screamed from the trees. And then one day Sharon too was gone. She had run off with another Mexican from town. Bobby was stoic about it. He shrugged and headed back to Los Angeles to start over again.

The old hacienda lay empty. Waiting. Beckoning us. Offering a crazy solution to our catastrophic financial woes.

11

So we put our house up for sale and rented the hacienda across the street. The one abandoned by Betsy. And Ken. And Sharon. And Bobby. It was a bittersweet moment. Bitter for me, who had built all the amenities of our first home lovingly with my own hands and hoped someday to return. Sweet for Charlize because it would buy us another year in Mexico, even after we payed off the mortgage and split the profits with our neighbors in Berkeley, who had since migrated to Portland in pursuit of promising career plans and abandoned their Mexican dream.

We began fixing up the main hacienda by re-coating the dull walls, inside and out, with the fresh white lime-and-chalk whitewash the Mexicans call *cal*. By replacing the tattered screens and a few broken windows. By replacing the frayed wiring that hung from loose staples on the walls. By trimming back the encroaching vegetation. By sweeping and dusting and hauling away the accumulated trash. And by polishing those worn red tiles with a mop and water with a splash of petroleo. Manuel helped tame the garden. Ophelia helped restore the house.

We had priced our old house for a quick sale, and it sold quickly. Even so, the paperwork required three trips to the Notary in Guadalajara and the proceeds were not released to our account for what seemed like months. The money was less than we had hoped, but enough to survive on for a while. We had to let Manuel and Ophelia go. We couldn't afford them any longer. And without them, something seemed to go out of our lives.

We discovered an abandoned adobe casita hidden in a grove of lemon trees and converted it into a *caballeriza* for Lucera. The property provided for all our needs. But there was an emptiness there. A loneliness. At night the rooms felt disconnected. In the dark you could sometimes hear the waves slapping the rocks on the beach. We would light the room we were in and let the spirits have the run of the others.

In June the rains came and settled the dust. The days were cooler. In the mornings Charlize rode her horse. I moved my writing into an unfinished spare bedroom. Charlize worked at the telares in the afternoon. I sat in the real estate office and read the newspapers. I played basketball and chess and took Pancho for long walks into the hills. We shopped at the markets every day. We chatted with our friends at the ice cream parlor. Friends from California flew down to see our new digs. In the afternoon we sat in the shade of a mango and watched the silver waters on the lake and the pale, distant desert mountains rising on the other side. It seemed to me we were like passengers at an airport, waiting for our final flight to depart.

12

One fall day, sometime after the rains had stopped and the fragrant bougainvillea was in bloom, Charlize failed to return from her horseback ride. It was beginning to grow dark and the hacienda felt hollow and empty. I rooted around in the kitchen for something to eat. This was not like her. Maybe she had fallen off her horse and was lying hurt somewhere. Or maybe it was something more sinister. I tried to put those thoughts out of my mind, but I couldn't. Just as I was preparing to go out in search, I heard the chain on the gate jangle and Charlize led Lucera into the yard.

"Are you all right?" I asked. "I was worried about you."

"I'm okay." She reached down to the horse's right foreleg. "Lucera threw a shoe. Up on the mountain. I had to walk her back down to the farrier and get it replaced."

"Were you by yourself?"

"Anita was with me." She turned and led the horse back to the tack shed to remove the saddle and feed and curry her. It all seemed to take a long time. Full darkness had fallen by the time she returned to the kitchen.

"You sure you're alright?" I asked again.

"Fine. How about some tacos?"

We ate in silence. Something was on her mind. I would wait until she was ready to talk about it. That night Charlize was uncharacteristically aggressive in bed. I did not know what to make of it, but somehow it felt ominous.

I did not sleep well that night, but the next morning everything seemed clearer as we followed our usual routines. The sunlight had a wonderful cleansing effect. Before leaving for her morning ride, Charlize called to me, "Don't forget that we have that party at the Joneses tonight."

"The Joneses?"

"Yeah, they're that new couple in the house up on Ocampo. We met them at the market, remember? I'm dying to see how they've fixed the place up."

"What time?"

"After dinner, I guess. It's an open house."

I was not feeling particularly game that evening. Still brooding, perhaps, over Charlize's mysterious late arrival home the night before. After a couple of quick shots of tequila, which didn't seem to improve my mood, I chatted with the host and hostess and listened to their stories that I didn't really care much about, just passing the time until we could go home and maybe get things sorted out. I remember the sweet smell of mesquite firewood from the *chiminea* on the outdoor brick patio. A mariachi band was playing beneath the broad leaves of the banana trees. A few people danced dreamily. I looked around at the expensive wrought iron furniture and the table spread with Mexican cuisine and the brick arches and the brick walls and the jabbering guests. I couldn't see Charlize anywhere.

Then I glanced up to the brick-walled balcony overlooking the festivities, and there she was, leaning over the railing beside a slender young man who had his arm around her waist. They saw me, and he quickly withdrew his arm and opened a space between them. Suddenly something choked in my chest and I felt light-headed and my breath came short and my heart was pounding and a cold sweat prickled my arms and neck. I couldn't believe what I was seeing. I didn't want this to be happening, whatever it was.

My eyes found an arch with a brick staircase inside rising toward the balcony. The noise and clatter of the party seemed to recede like an ocean wave shushing away on the sand. My whole being was focused on that stairway. Without willing it, my feet carried me across the patio, oblivious to the milling crowd, and began to climb the curving stairs. At the top I found the door onto the patio. Charlize and her friend had turned with their backs to the brick wall to watch me arrive. I stepped through the doorway.

The fellow was thin and sallow and nondescript, by appearance younger than either of us. He moved nervously away from Charlize, before realizing he had placed himself in front of the low railing with a ten-foot drop to the brick patio below. So he quickly reversed course and edged behind her toward the door. I let him pass.

"What's going on?" I heard myself asking Charlize.

"What does it look like," she responded, her lips pursed in defiance. Haughty.

"I'll just give you two some space," said the inconsequential young man as he disappeared out the doorway.

"That's who you were with yesterday," I said. "Isn't it?"

"Yes." Her eyes blazed, unafraid.

"And the two of you . . . ?"

"Yes." There was no compassion in her eyes. No plea for forgiveness. She stood her ground. "So what?"

I didn't reach for her hand. Didn't try to lead her home. Didn't touch her at all. For that bewildering instant I was my father, or the person I imagined my father to be, and doing what my imagined father would have done. I said to her, "I'm going to have to leave you."

"You do what you have to do," was all she replied.

I don't recall descending those stairs or pushing my way through the crowd. In blind confusion I fled the fiesta, through the front gate, stumbling down onto the dark cobbles. A massive earthquake seemed to have rearranged the geography. Abrupt. Devastating. Nothing was recognizable. I was disoriented. Lost. I couldn't comprehend what was happening. Charlize was the fabric of my life. I loved her. I hated her. These were the warp and weft of my being.

But for instinct, I might not have made it back to the hacienda. With one foot following the other on those obscure and uneven cobbles, seeing nothing around me, I found my way to the iron gate where Pancho slept with his snout lying across the lower metal strap. He barked once before recognizing me, then jumped up and tried to insert his nose into my hand as I closed the gate behind me. Like a sleepwalker I led him into the kitchen and scooped a cup of kibble into his bowl, but he ignored it. Pancho sensed that something seismic had happened.

What was I going to do?

Pancho followed as I wandered from room to room, discovering an album Charlize loved and plates drying in the rack and a wall hanging from Oaxaca and her clothes folded across an old equipali chair. They all meant nothing anymore. Nothing. Meaning itself no longer made any sense. I could not seem to cry or laugh or scream out the pressure building inside. And I could not quench the overwhelming ache.

I sat on the veranda and rocked and waited for her to come home. Pancho waited with me, patiently, his chin on his paws, knowing something was dreadfully wrong. Fifteen minutes. An hour. I gave her time to sort things out in her own mind. Discover the right thing to do. In my mind I ran through the dialogue that would have to be said when she arrived. The imagined dialogue my imagined father would have uttered. I listened for the gate to open and clang shut. The night grew cold.

Shivering, I went inside and waited a second hour at the kitchen table with my head in my hands as hope drained out of me. Then I laid on the bed, fully clothed and ready for the impending confrontation, and tried to catch a little sleep. But it was no use. Real sleep would not come. Just swaths of dark delirium. I would doze, then wake up to a living nightmare from which I knew I would never fully awaken. Charlize had turned her back on me. Abandoned me. She to whom I had opened myself completely. She who knew me better than any other living soul. She had found me unworthy. Fled from me without a word. Without even enough respect to come home and talk over this obscenity that was taking place. She didn't care that it was over. She made no effort to try to make things right again.

Not that things could ever be made right again. The trust was broken. Humpty Dumpty lay in a million pieces at the foot of the wall, and I was eternally damned. Like this cursed hacienda. I gave up trying to sleep and walked out under the blazing stars. Familiar stars, but so remote and cold!

Everything else had grown unfamiliar. Of another time. Another place. An owl hooted from the direction of the lake, and for a moment I wondered if it might be a sign. But I knew it was no sign. It meant nothing. It just *was*. Meaningless and empty, like everything else, it just *was*.

This was not my land. These were not my people. I had no land. I had no people. And this ancient, brooding hacienda, lying like an open sore beside the lake, was not my home. I no longer had a home. Charlize had been my home.

Numbly I began to pack my things. Haphazardly. My clothing went into a suitcase. My toiletries into my shaving kit. Odds and ends into a cardboard box. Common things I used every day. *My* things. I began carrying them out to the station wagon and tossing them in the back with no sense of order or reason. Then I reconsidered and folded down the back seat to make room for my sleeping bag and a foam pad and shoved everything else to the other side. I would need to sleep somewhere.

Pancho followed me back and forth, his little whines asking if this was the right thing to be doing? Or all a mistake? But I didn't know what was right anymore.

This is what my father would have done. He knew what was right and what was wrong. And Charlize had been dead wrong. *I'm going to have to leave you*, I had said to her. *You do what you have to do*, she had replied. I was hemmed in by our words. My threat, her reply, both so quickly uttered. Thoughtless words. If she had come home then, things might have unfolded differently. But she did not come home, and that was the loudest statement of all. The die had been cast. I really had no choice.

Our important papers were in a dresser drawer, and I rifled through them. I shoved my visa and my passport and a few other records of my own affairs into a spare pillow case. Then I wrote myself a check for half the balance in our account and left the checkbook on the kitchen table.

One last time I walked through those rooms that had been my home, without, I now knew, ever really being my home. Looking one last time for things I should take with me from among all the other things I would leave behind forever. That was the hardest part. That's when the truth sank in. That's when I knew it was all over.

When I returned to the station wagon, my eyes were finally wet. Pancho was crouched down in the passenger seat, afraid I would leave him behind too. I could offer him no comfort. I would have to leave him. Charlize was the one who wanted a dog. As the sky began to lighten and the stars fade for the last time, I drove the station wagon out onto the cobblestone street. Then I led Pancho back inside, unhooked the leash, and closed the gate on him. He whimpered through the bars as I gazed back.

There was something *wrong* about that old hacienda. I could just make out from the cobblestones outside the wide prison gate, through the brick arch of the inner courtyard, the main house brooding like an unhealed wound in the ghostly gloaming. Something broken and dark and sinister lurked beneath the cracking plaster and crumbling mortar that bound together those ancient adobe blocks.

Pancho's sad brown eyes held mine through the squares of cold iron. How could I leave him behind, they asked? *I* was his master. His protector. His dearest friend. *I* had trained him, not Charlize. Reason and emotion tore at each other. I would be on the run. What was I going to do with a big dog? Yet how could I leave him there in that abominable hacienda?

In the end, I just couldn't do it. So one last time I pushed open the gate and drew it closed forever as Pancho scrambled into the station wagon for the long, painful journey with me into a new country that I could not begin to comprehend.

Cover Crop

Every night, Blind Mori accompanies me in song.
Under the covers, two mandarin ducks whisper to each other.
We promise to be together forever,
But right now this old fellow enjoys an eternal spring.
  – Ikkyū (1394-1481) translated by John Stevens

1

I awaken to the tinkling of a bell as it is carried through the dimly-lit zendo. Without hesitation I arise, fold my mat and my blanket and stow them in the cabinet before me, set out my zafu, and remove my tooth-brush, toothpaste, and threadbare towel. All about me I hear the rustling of other monks doing the same.

In the lavatory I await my turn for a sink and a toilet stall. There are no mirrors above the sinks. Harsh light glares from the bare fluorescent bulb in the center of the ceiling. The morning is cold. No one speaks. Aimless chit-chat is discouraged, and that suits me just fine, particularly on a morning when the divide between dream and wakefulness is so fragile. As I finish blotting the cold water from my face, I feel a tug on my sleeve.

I turn to find Roshi Koshin hovering beside me, his shaven head hidden by the hood of his cloak and his thin lips tinted blue from the cold. Half my stature, slender and slight, he bows in gasshō and whispers in his Irish brogue, "Can ye help bring in firewood?"

"Of course," I reply. We bow to each other.

As I step outside, a cold breeze gusting from the north cuts through my robe. The brightening sky illuminates the looming western face of Mt. Shasta, all draped in snow down to timberline. For a moment, my eyes linger there. I love the mountain. In its lee to the south, haloed by the seminal pink glow where the sun will rise, floats one of those odd lenticular clouds, just beginning to form like a tiny seed that will mushroom into a saucer of swirling vapors as the day warms. *The mountain makes it own weather*, I think.

I find the roshi bending over one of the neat stacks of fragrant incense cedar that line the cloistered walkway and help him fill his arms with sticks split as fine as kindling. I fill my arms too, and silently we carry our burdens inside the warm kitchen, where breakfast preparation has already begun. The aroma of fresh-baked bread makes my stomach churn. After two more loads, he bows to me. I bow and return silently to the darkened zendo.

Beside my cabinet, barely visible in the dim light of the altar lanterns, I plump up my zafu, lift the skirts of my robe, and carefully settle cross-legged onto the cushion facing the wall, letting my robe drape over my legs and feet. Slowly I sway from side to side, back and forth, in a spiral of decreasing circles until I feel squarely grounded. I fold my hands in my lap to form the mudra of meditation, draw a slow, deep breath, and allow my eyes to half-close, unfocused on the thin baseboard of the wall before me. Around me I hear the purr of trainees reciting their kesa verse. As a layman, I have no kesa. I wait. I breathe. It always begins with waiting. Breathing. In time, a bell rings, a chime struck purely, clearly, once, twice, a third time, and all is silence. I breathe. I allow my mind to quiet.

The most difficult part is the thoughts. They come unbidden. Unceasingly. The images. The thoughts. And I try to let them go as they come. Let them pass on without attachment. Each demands my attention. But I let it go. And another takes its place. Like the tide. Like the internal rhythm of an eternal surf. A surf that swirls around the ribs of a wrecked ship . . . .

I have been at the abbey for months, a refuge from a shipwrecked life. In my memory and in my mind's eye, the bare-boned ribs of a broken vessel emerge from the pounding surf while the jetsam and flotsam of a broken life and wasted years wash endlessly back and forth in the shallows. At the whim of the waves and the tide. The abbey is my island, my refuge, my shelter in the storm—

I return to the present. Begin again, breathing deeply, counting the breaths. One . . . Two . . . Three . . . .

I have been at the abbey for many months as a layman, between worlds, and I fear that they are beginning to wonder if I will ever make the commitment. Make the commitment that they have all made. The commitment to receive the ten precepts in the Jūkai ceremony, shave my head, vow celibacy, and become a priest-trainee on the road to ordination. How does one decide such a thing?

Again my mind has wandered. I draw another deep breath. Straighten my spine. Settle my shoulders. Relax my diaphragm. Breathe through my belly. Breathe again. Begin again to count my breaths. One . . . Two . . . Three . . . Four . . . .

Like a dog chasing its tail. I picture the dog, circling one way and then the other. My thoughts are like a dog chasing its tail. I suppress a smile—

And I begin again. Breathing. Counting . . . .

Yesterday a young laymen named Chris told me he had felt the presence of the Ancestors in the darkened zendo the night before. It had moved him deeply. He was ready to receive the precepts. Commit himself to following the Buddha's Way. Fifteen-years younger than I, he valued my opinion. I did not know what to say to him. I have never felt the presence of the Ancestors—

I draw myself back. Settle myself. Begin again. Breathe. Begin to count.

Suddenly I become aware of thoughts that are not my own. They scurry like inhuman things, like rodents through an alley, searching for something. They have always scurried, of course, my thoughts, but these don't belong here. There is something strange in them. In these alien thoughts. Things I never learned. Things I never experienced. Things not of this earth. Not voices. Mad men hear voices, and I am not mad. No, these are *someone else's thoughts* that have strayed into my mind. Thoughts I should not be seeing . . . .

The sky at night. A chart of unknown stars. But the unfamiliar chart seems familiar somehow. And I feel a longing to return to a place too alien to grasp or describe. Sand swirls across lifeless dunes. A sun blazes too yellow against a magenta sky. In the distance rises a crimson tower. It is a place I do not understand. A place that makes no sense to me. But I feel it anyway. I am drawn to it. And I long for it. I feel it and

I perceive it and I long for it. But I do not understand it. My purpose here is–

A bell rings sharply, a single pure tone of release and loss, signaling the end of zazen. Monks shuffle about me, bowing to their cushions. Bowing to the fellowship. Bowing to the Buddha. They form ranks facing the altar in the open center of the zendo. Each has his place for the morning service. Shaken by the images I have seen, I am slow to join them. Slow to take my place. The disciplinarian waits for me, then intones, "The Scripture of Kanzeon Bosatsu." A gong sounds, and the monks begin a mindful chant of the scripture amid the scent of incense and the soft glow of candle light.

But my mind is elsewhere. As I mouth the familiar verses, I wonder at the visions I have seen and the loneliness and longing I just felt. They seemed so real. They *are* real, I am convinced.

2

The abbey has plans to expand the dining hall so that all the priests and trainees can eat together. But for now, lay trainees and neophyte monks must wait for the second breakfast sitting. While we wait, temple cleanup follows the morning service for us. Chris and I have been assigned to clean the common room of the large stone building, where the senior monks stay. The abbey was once a motel, before the interstate rerouted traffic, and its dozen beautiful stone structures were the first to be inhabited for the monastery.

Chris sweeps the floor while I dust and tidy up the tables and chairs. A television set, rarely used, has been turned toward the wall and covered by a blanket. On top a local newspaper lies folded, and my eye catches a partial headline. I unfold the paper. "Lenticular Clouds Caused By Global Warming," it reads. I scan snippets through the article. "Climate change is causing more frequent extreme weather phenomena . . . intensifying natural variances . . . not clear what is cause and effect . . . trend expected to continue . . . ."

Chris is standing beside me, reading too. Though in his early twenties, his pale cheeks still show the scars of acne. His short reddish-brown hair is tightly curled. He looks away to blow his nose into a

Kleenex, but I have already seen something in his eyes that wasn't there yesterday.

"What is it, Chris?" I ask softly.

But Chris is unsure of himself. Perhaps a little unsettled. Unsettled just like me, I guess, and like me afraid to say anything that would sound too crazy. "Nothing," he mutters, and resumes sweeping beneath the table.

I move the chairs for him and gaze out the window. The morning sun casts its orange-red glow on the bottom of the saucer-shaped cloud hovering beside Mt. Shasta. The lenticular phantasm. Crepuscular. Like a roused cat. On the sidewalk outside Roshi Koshin and another monk are staring up at the cloud's pink glow.

"Something's on your mind," I press.

Chris snorts. Perhaps it was my choice of words. But he has nothing to say. He just watches my eyes. To see what might be coming next.

"You saw it, too," I whisper. It was not a question. "The sand. The tower. The chart."

Chris glances around to see if anybody is listening. No one is there. He turns back and nods. Just a slight dip of the head.

"What was it?" I ask.

He shakes his head.

I ponder for a moment, then assure him, "This is *not* the Ancestors, Chris."

He nods, perhaps a little relieved, then resumes sweeping. I watch in silence for a long while before he says, "Those clouds, maybe?"

3

During breakfast I feel a hand touch my shoulder and a voice whispers my name. I turn and am startled to find the dark eyes of Suzanne, a striking young woman whom I have watched from across the room at classes morning and afternoon for the past few weeks. I feel like I know her, though we have never spoken. She bows in gasshō, her face inches from my own. In a glance I take in her face. The beauty of her pale, delicate features. Turned up nose. Black lashes. Straight black hair in a short pixie cut. As a layman trainee, she has not yet shaved her head. Two small birthmarks above her right cheekbone remind me of a snakebite. Her neck is a smooth white arc emerging from her dark robe. I breathe in the faint scent of soap. Her serious lips are pressed together in concentration on her task.

I swivel clumsily, scraping my chair, and return her bow. She raises those piercing eyes and hands me a note. I take it, and we bow to each other again. Then she rises and glides out of the dining hall.

My heart is thudding as I return to my oatmeal. With my knife I cut the seal and unfold the sheet of paper. It is a handwritten note from Roshi Koshin bidding me to come see him at his room as soon as breakfast is over. *Odd*, I think. *I'm not scheduled for a personal audience with him for another day. Something must have changed.* But I see it as an excellent chance to discuss with him the strange visions that Chris and I experienced this morning during zazen.

I follow the flagstone pathway and find his room in one of the old motel buildings. His door is closed. I knock once.

"Enter," he says.

Roshi Koshin is seated on his cushion on a raised mat at the far end of the small chamber, facing the door, waiting for me. I step inside, close the door behind me, and kneel before him on the carpet. I bow in gasshō. He returns the bow, then gestures to a zafu. I pull the cushion over and settle myself facing him. Seated formally above me, he appears larger and more imposing than he did when I loaded his arms with firewood earlier that morning. His shaved head and sashed temple robe convey an austere gravity, but his face is soft and peaceful, his eyes gentle as they study me. I drop my gaze, and we are both silent for a long time.

"How is yer practice a'coming?" he asks at last.

I never know how to answer such a question. I shift a bit. "I keep trying," I grin as lightheartedly as I can manage.

But this is not a lighthearted moment. He does not smile back. "Have ye given any more thought to receivin' the precepts? Takin' Jūkai? Becomin' a priest?"

"I've thought about it," I mumble, lowering my eyes again. "It's just that . . . " I gaze up at him, "I don't think I'm ready . . . yet."

He nods. Considers what he is going to say for a moment, then asks, "Why are ye here?" There is no irony intended. It is not an accusation. He honestly wants to know.

The question touches something deep inside me. It is a question I myself would like an answer to. But I have none. I shake my head. "I don't know," I manage. We are both silent for a time, and then I add, "Maybe because I have no place else to be."

He smiles at last. Nods. "'Tis not a proper reason for ye t'be here," he says. "And ye know it."

It is my turn to nod. We are both silent for a long time, wondering what the consequences will be. What to do about the situation.

"I appreciate yer honesty," he says at last. "I think ye would make a foyne priest." Then he draws a sharp breath and says, "The Abbess spoke t'me this mornin'."

I wait for more.

"She asked me about ye."

"About me? I didn't think she knew I existed."

"She said we're going to have to ask ye to leave the abbey."

I am shocked. The foundations of my world are shaken. "Leave?" I manage. "Why?"

"T'make room. Room for those who seriously desire t'follow the path to priesthood."

I cannot speak.

"Her own words were, ''Tis not a country club.'"

I shake my head to clear it. It is of no use. "When?"

"Tomorrow. When ye can get yer things together. I'll have Suzanne give ye a lift into town after mornin' service." He falls silent.

I nod dumbly. My head spins.

"And when ye're ready t'take the vows, ye may return."

"I can come back?"

"Aye. Of course. When ye're ready. I would like that. We've become friends, don't ye think? And I believe with all my heart that ye would make a foyne priest."

I fight back tears.

"When ye're ready," he repeats reassuringly. "Ye can come back."

4

Everything has lost meaning. The morning dharma class drags past like an empty pantomime. I hear nothing. *Where will I go? What will I do? How will I pass the time?* I plod on through the day, seeing it all with different eyes. I split firewood. Eat a meal. Pound on a buried rock with an iron bar. Sit through another class. Chant sutras. Eat another meal. But the gestures have become hollow. The hall, the rock walls, the cloister are all cardboard stage flats. The monks are actors in a theater production without a plot. My mind is elsewhere. Empty. I do not understand.

At the evening meditation I settle myself woodenly on my cushion, expecting nothing. I wonder how I will endure these final vespers. I cross my legs. Straighten my back. Lower my abdomen. Relax my shoulders. I breathe . . . and I breathe . . . and suddenly, unexpectedly, peace comes upon me. It saturates my breathing. It is in my heartbeat. Calm infuses me. Without breathing, I breathe. There is no need to count. A joy springs up. Inwardly I smile. I am free. As a man condemned to die is finally free. My mind is empty. There are no visions of star travelers. No thought for what tomorrow will bring. I breathe on my cushion and there is nothing more than this.

Too soon the bell rings. We stand and bow three times and form lines with our hands in gasshō. The disciplinarian intones, "The Litany of the Great Compassionate One," and a gong sounds. I am fully awake, riding the crest of the black-robed wave as it begins to chant for the first and final time:

Adoration to the Triple Treasure!
Adoration to Kanzeon Who is the Great Compassionate One!
Om, to the One who leaps beyond all fear!
Having adored Him, may I enter into the heart of the Noble,
Adored Kanzeon!
His life is the completion of meaning;
it is pure; it is that which makes all beings victorious
and cleanses the path of all existence . . . .

Something clicks inside my head. I stop chanting and repeat the phrase, "and cleanses the path of all existence." The trainees on each side glance at me, but they go on chanting. It is like I have awakened. But not to enlightenment. No, not to satori. But to something far more sanguinary. *A blood red tower.* And suddenly the star charts and the blowing dunes and the red tower make a sort of crazy sense.

The moment passes, as all moments do. And then service is over. I am empty and alone. I store away my zafu. Spread out my sleeping mat. My feet find their way into the lavatory, where I speak to no one. I have not spoken since my meeting with the roshi. I am afraid. Ashamed. I dwell on what will happen tomorrow.

5

When the service is well underway the following morning, the visions are back . . . .

Home. A longing to return. A desert world of billowing sand. A red tower. A star map. A route. An emptiness–

The great hall grows restless. A chair squeaks. Someone coughs. Another blows her nose softly. Monks shift their positions. I abandon trying to meditate. Withdraw from the visions. Give up trying to understand them. *Where will I go?* I wonder instead.

After morning service I find my way into the storage room and pull down the cardboard box with my name printed on one end. I unfold the interlaced flaps and remove my flattened duffle bag. Carefully I remove my khaki trousers. My red-checked flannel shirt. My worn engineer's boots. My wool jacket. A plastic freezer bag holds my wallet with twenty-two dollars in cash, my checkbook, small change, a chapstick, the keys to an automobile I no longer own, and the front door key to an apartment where I am no longer welcome. I pull out extra underwear, two T-shirts, a pair of wool socks, and a handkerchief. At the bottom lies a thin manila folder.

I remove my robe and pull on my civilian clothing. The robe I fold. It is not mine. It belongs to the abbey. But I like it and will take it. I lay the robe in the bottom of my duffle. By automatic funds transfer I have established a small monthly endowment designed to cover my board and lodging at the abbey. The fund will pay for dozens of new robes. I examine the rest of my possessions as if they belong to someone else.

They don't amount to much. None of it interests me. I stuff it all into the duffle.

Tossed back into the river of life, I think as I wind my way toward the front gate. *To see if I will sink or swim. To see if I will find my way.* I smile inwardly. *It's all a part of the training.* The front office is locked. There is no one to say goodbye to. I close the chain-link gate behind me.

Outside a white pickup idles, all dinged and battered and scraped, water vapor puffing from its tailpipe. I can see Suzanne's dark outline behind the wheel. I dump my duffle bag and zafu into the bed and wrench open the creaking door. I begin to bow, think better of it, and climb onto the worn passenger seat. It is warm inside. I rub my hands together over the heater vent. "Thanks for the ride," I say.

"Where can I take you?" she asks brusquely, grinding the floor shift into first and easing off the clutch. Like me, she is dressed in civilian clothes, a bulky orange down sweater over her denim dungarees.

"Is there a Denny's nearby?"

"I'll take you to the Black Bear Diner."

"That would be fine," I tell her. "Have you eaten?"

She shakes her head.

"Well, how about if I buy you breakfast?"

In low gear we wind down the access road in silence. Trying not to stare at her, I gaze through my fogging side window. The forest slips past. A farm field opens, green and damp. Beyond it a sign reads, "Cascade Growers Co-Op. Fertilizer. Hydroponic Supplies. Cover Crops." It gives an address. "Cover Crops" sticks in my mind as the forest curtain closes and the sign disappears.

The rattling truck accelerates up the freeway ramp heading south. Over the roar of the engine she says, "So you're leaving the monastery."

I turn to her. Think about how to put it. Then reply, "They asked me to leave."

"Why?"

Again I consider. "I told them I'm not ready to make the commitment," I say. "To receive the precepts." I consider how much to tell her. "The Abbess wants to make room for those who are."

She glances over, considers me silently. "I think I know where you're coming from."

That surprises me. "So you're having trouble making a commitment, too?" I ask.

She bobs her head. "I'm still testing the waters. How long have you been there?"

"Seems like forever."

In Mt. Shasta City she pulls into the half-filled lot of the Black Bear Diner. Our breaths steam in the gusts of cold, damp air. I hold the front door for her. The waitress leads us to a booth in the big front window. Suzanne tugs off her bright sweater before sliding in. Beneath it a formless gray fleece shirt covers her slim shoulders. I try not to stare. Neither of us look at the menu. She orders a fruit bowl, toast, and a cup of coffee. I order scrambled egg-whites, toast, and decaf. We sit there silently facing each other across the damp table. "Excuse me," she says and bounces out to the women's room.

Outside the window Mt. Shasta floats like an imposing white ghost. In its lee hovers the saucer shape of a new cloud, its puffy bottom glowing golden in the rising sunlight. *Lenticular.* I gaze around the restaurant. It's been a long time since I've been in the outside world. Everything is artificial. The orange naugahyde seats. The vinyl table tops. Plastic picture menus. It all seems so strange. The clatter of dishes and ceaseless chatter of the patrons are a corrosive surf pounding my ears. Unwelcome. Eroding my inner calm. Everyone is animated, talking and gesticulating, like tendrils of vetch dancing in the breeze. "Cover crop" pops into my head again. For some odd reason I see all of the patrons as a waving cover crop. I am not sure what that means.

My hands settle in my lap and form themselves into a circle. The mudra of meditation. I take a deep breath. Press the air deep into my belly. Let it out. Half close my eyes. Breathe . . . .

Lenticular clouds. A cover crop. Cleansing the path. A red tower—

Suzanne slides back into the booth just as the coffee and breakfast arrive. We eat in silence. My eyes are downcast, on my food, but I sense her gazing at me.

"You were watching me," she says causally. "During class."

I stir sweetener into my coffee. Take a sip. "Yes."

"Why?" Her dark eyes peer into my soul.

What can I say? "I thought you were pretty."

Her stern expression relaxes. She smiles. She leans back against the naugahyde. "You never said much in class."

"No," I reply. "I was there to listen." I take a bite of toast. Chew. "Neither did you."

She considers me, then says out of the blue, "You've seen them, haven't you?"

I look up into her eyes.

"During morning meditation," she adds.

I know what she means. "Yes," I say. "The tower."

She nods.

"The dunes."

She nods again.

"The . . . *longing*."

"To go home," she confirms. Sips her coffee. "What do you think it means?"

I shake my head. Take a bite of eggs. A bite of toast. Chew. Sip my decaf. "I think they're something . . . something we're not supposed to be seeing."

"A communication," she ponders. "A message. Maybe. But from whom?"

I sigh. She is drawing out a crazy notion that I have been keeping buried. "The Farmers."

She considers. "The *Farmers*?" She swallows a spoonful of fruit. "What is *that* supposed to mean?"

I smile at her directness. "Maybe 'farmers' is the wrong word. How about 'caretakers'? Or just 'observers'? I haven't really thought this through yet. I'm sorry. It's just a crazy notion."

Her eyes bore into me. "But it *feels right*, doesn't it? Go on. I'll tell you how crazy it sounds."

I shake my head. "I can't. I'm not ready yet."

She finishes her fruit bowl. Her toast. Drains her coffee cup and nests the dishes on the table. Dabs up a coffee spill with her napkin. "Where will you go?" she asks.

I take a breath. "I don't know." I think about it. "I guess I'll buy a bus ticket for Redding. After that . . . I don't know."

We gaze at our hands as the waitress gathers the plates and leaves the check.

"I have to tell you something," she says.

"What's that?"

"I was watching you, too."

I am pleasantly surprised. My grin feels a little lopsided. "Really?"

"Are you gay?" she asks suddenly.

"No!" I snort. "I've been married. Twice, as a matter of fact. It just didn't work out for me. Either time. Wrong person. Wrong time. Wrong place. But not because I was gay. Why do you ask?"

She considers. "I've got an extra bed at my place. A small apartment right here in Mt. Shasta. You're welcome to stay there for a few days while you sort things out."

"Are you?"

"What?"

"Are you . . . lesbian?"

"No. Heavens, no. Well, I mean, I *have* . . . you know– " She breaks off, flustered as a young girl. Redness creeps into the pale flesh around the bridge of her nose. Spreads into her cheeks. "I mean, no. I don't think I am, really. I mean, isn't that why I asked you . . . about– "

"How old are you?" I interrupt mercifully.

"Twenty-nine. I'll be thirty next month." She is glad the subject has changed.

"Old enough to know better," I grin. I lean back to consider my options. Think them through. There really aren't any. I examine her intently. Her pretty face. Her short-cropped hair. The birthmark on her cheek. The curve of her pale neck. She is a lovely woman. She can do better than me. I take a deep breath. Let it out.

"What?" she demands.

"Did Roshi Koshin put you up to this?"

"No!" She protests, then reconsiders. "Well . . . he *did* ask me to do what I could for you. He thinks the world of you, you know. But, no, he . . . he didn't suggest that I do anything in particular."

"Then why are you inviting me into your home?" I ask.

She drops her eyes. Breathes. Recovers her poise. Looks up and smiles. "Why don't we just say . . . let's just say that maybe I want to hear what you think is going on with all those crazy visions we've been having."

6

Her apartment is a small walkup at the top of a rickety set of outside wooden stairs. It is the converted top floor of an ancient, dilapidated Victorian a few blocks from the main drag. She leaves her shoes by the front door, and I do the same. The inside is clean and neat and exudes the musty odor of old books and spice tea. The small front room is carpeted and furnished with a worn sofa, a chair, and a floor lamp. No television. An old Navajo blanket is draped over the sofa. Suzanne doesn't own much stuff. She shows me through the kitchen to a tiny back bedroom, not much bigger than a closet. An open futon covers most of a worn beige carpet. There is just enough room for a table lamp, an orange crate, and a couple of cardboard boxes stacked in a corner. A small, high window opens toward the west. There is no view of the mountain. It suits me fine. I set down my duffle bag and center my zafu on the futon.

In the hall she clicks a thermostat, and a gas heater whooshes to life and begins to crackle and creak. She pokes her head in and asks, "Will this do?"

"Perfectly." I bow in gratitude.

"Listen, I have to get to work," she tells me. "I'm a little late already."

"What do you do?" I follow her into the hall.

"Oh, I'm a phlebotomist. On-call part time at the hospital. The regular tech is out on family leave today ." She turns to see whether further explanation is needed.

"You draw blood from people," I say.

She smiles. "I do. For lab work, mostly. I have to change now." She ducks into her bedroom and shuts the door. When she emerges, she is wearing green scrubs with a name tag and photo ID clipped above her breast.

"When will you be back?" I ask.

"Not until after six." She pulls on a navy windbreaker and drags open the front door.

"I can make soup for dinner," I offer. "If you trust me in your kitchen."

"That would be nice," she smiles. "And I do." The door closes behind her.

I stare at the closed door for a long time. Little squares of glass behind the sheer mesh curtain let in a diffuse, dreamy light. I draw a deep breath. Let it out. Drawn another. Let it out. Now what?

I decide to try meditating. In my room I settle myself on the zafu. I stay in my civies. No sense changing if I have to go out to the market later. I sit. I breathe. I try to count my breaths, but they are slippery this morning. They wriggle away and I lose count, again and again. This is not the abbey. Not a proper zendo. It shouldn't make any difference, but it does. No bells. No incense. No chanting. No sangha. No fellow monks sweating white beads beside me. My thoughts wander over my new surroundings. I am not used to this strange bright room. My situation. I try again. I breathe . . . .

A loop of dark hair curls forward under Suzanne's ear. The twin pricks of the serpent's fangs mark her cheek. The curve of her neck. I want to touch the curve–

I draw myself back into the present. Shift my posture. Bear down harder. Begin again. Breathe. Breathe again. Begin to count my breaths . . . .

Say the wrong thing, and a gap opens up between heaven and earth. Do the wrong thing and a gap opens. A gap of years. Thirty years old. Forty-one. A gap of eleven years opens. A gap opens up between–

I try to bring myself back into the present. Again and again. It is no use. I give up and wander about the apartment, looking over Suzanne's possessions to see who she might be. In the kitchen I think about dinner and pull a large pot out of a lower cupboard. As I look through the drawers for cooking implements, I practice breathing. Practice bringing myself back to the present.

I step into her bedroom. Her fresh scent lingers on top of the dry, spicy ambiance of the old Victorian. A poster of a mandala is mounted on the wall above her low bed. The bed is neatly made and covered with a striped wool blanket. A quilt is folded over the foot. A big double-hung window faces east. A faded paisley curtain is drawn aside. From her pillow she can see Mt. Shasta through the wavy Victorian glass. The mountain looms white over the roof of an outbuilding and the bare branches of an ancient apple tree. Against the wall stands a chest of drawers. Beside it is a coffee table with a small wooden Buddha and her incense burner, a rice bowl half-filled with sand and bristling with spent sticks. In one corner a straight-back chair holds her folded clothes. Beneath it is her zafu. Clothes hang in an open closet. A short bookshelf is half-filled with books. I do not read the titles. That would feel like intruding. On a little round nightstand is a short lamp, a digital clock, and a small volume she is reading. There is no computer. No television. No knickknacks. No photos. Her private life appears to be as transient as my own.

I pick up the book beside her bed. It is thin and narrow. Entitled "Wild Ways," it is a book of Zen verses by Ikkyū translated by John Stevens. I think I might have heard the name Ikkyū, but I am not sure. Not at the abbey. I read the translator's introduction. Ikkyū was a Rinzai Zen monk, an iconoclast, and a reluctant abbot. Sometimes a wastrel. Sometimes a saint. He would cast off his robes and leave the monastery for long periods to practice his Zen in the taverns and brothels of the wide world, drinking, whoring, eating animal flesh, and breaking every precept. In a straw hat, raincoat, and sandals he would live among the fish mongers and farmers, sometimes under a bridge, and sometimes as a hermit in the deep forest. He called himself "Crazy Cloud" and scribed his beautiful poems as he wandered his own Zen path. Many verses described his joyous lovemaking with the blind courtesan, Lady Mori, who came to him when he was already an old man. Yet he had followers who recognized him as a great Zen master. When he was eighty years old, they called him back to become the abbot at Diatoku-ji Monastery. Of that he wrote, "I hate the smell of incense."

I sit down on the carpet and lean my back against the doorway. I begin to read the poems. They speak to me. I read them all, from start to finish, then move onto the sofa in the front room and read them all again. Only then can I return the slim volume to Suzanne's bedside table.

7

I stroll down to the business district. It is only a few blocks from the apartment. The warm sun feels good on my face. Mt. Shasta Boulevard is busy with traffic. Everyone seems to be in a hurry. Waves of roaring vehicles wash past ceaselessly from either direction. The air is hazy with fumes. Only a few people move along the sidewalk. Out of their vehicles, walking, they look soft and vulnerable, like grubs. We nod to each other as we pass. I suppress an urge to bow.

I find the bank. I have been here before, but it seems like such a long time ago. In another life. It is an attractive structure. A monument with tall, exposed-aggregate walls topped with narrow strips of glass that leaves the impression the roof is floating. It is a temple of its own kind. No one else seems to notice. I go inside to the marble counter and write a check for cash. I breathe deeply as I wait in line for the window. The teller is too cheerful. Too friendly. She needs to see my ID and seems to recognize me in the photo. I do not. I ask to check my account balance and am comfortable with it. Money flowed in. Now it flows out. Like the air we breathe. It will flow in again. I cash the check, the teller counts out twenties, and I fold them into my wallet without counting again.

After the bank I stop at the library and look something up about dinosaurs in the reference encyclopedia. When I finally arrive at the market, it becomes almost too much for me. The bright yellow and red boxes crowding the shelves. The harsh fluorescent lighting. The gleaming floors and chrome-edge cold cases. The mindless chattering and bustle of shoppers. A sea of samsara. I shop as efficiently as I can, letting my breathing buoy me like a life vest, then flee with paper bags clutched in both arms.

When I get back to the apartment, I sit and breathe at the kitchen table before eating a chunk of tofu and a slice of bread. I boil some water for tea as I set out the groceries, trying to remain in the present. Aware. My fingers trace the grain of the oiled wood as I place the cutting board carefully on the counter. I breathe. I feel the knife handle. There is nowhere else I would rather be. One by one I wash the carrots in cool water. Breathe as I cut each one. Wash the celery. Slice each stalk.

Dice each slice. Breathe. Chop up a slice of onion. Cut some broccoli and cauliflower. Toss it all into the pot and add vegetable broth and water. Pause. Breathe. I open a can of white beans, dump it into the pot, put it on low to simmer, and stir in barley and lentils. I turn down the heat.

While the soup cooks, I strip off my clothing in the bathroom. In the mirror I do not recognize my face. I dig my shaving kit out of my duffle bag and find a towel neatly folded in the hall cupboard. Mindfully I shower and shave. When I gaze again into the fog-streaked mirror, I appear both younger and older than I remember. I blot my hair with the towel and pull on my drawstring meditation pants and the purloined black robe.

I stir the soup, taste it, and add seasoning. I try meditating again, but it is no good. I need to sort things out. I need to figure out what I am going to tell Suzanne when the time comes, as it surely will. About the visions. My crazy notion. I stir the soup again and turn the heat up a bit. Find a yellow pad and a pen. Wait for inspiration. Stir the soup. *Lenticular clouds. The red tower. A cover crop. Cleansing the path.* Those are all a part of it, but I try to remember what I saw *behind* those images. What I saw in the mind of . . . of whoever was doing the dreaming. *A longing for home. A purpose for being here.* It seems crazier than ever when I try to write it down.

Suzanne is weary when she gets home. She washes up and changes into her own meditation robe. Her white skin is lovely against the black cloth. I serve the soup in shallow bowls at the kitchen table. Through the window the sun sinks behind the Klamath Mountains. The room darkens, but we do not turn on the light. Like at the abbey, we eat in silence.

8

"Tell me about the visions," she says after the dishes are done. She settles onto the sofa and drapes her meditation robe over her curled legs. "You called them 'Farmers'."

I pace back and forth uncomfortably. This is all speculation, what I have to say. A fantasy. Madness. But in the end I sigh and face her squarely. "Sixty-three million years ago," I begin, "these . . . Farmers . . .

or whatever you want to call them . . . chanced upon the earth. It was just one planet among billions . . . circling one star among trillions. But it had potential.   It was located precisely in the right place.   Except the atmosphere was poisonous. At least for them it was poisonous. But that was something that could be adjusted. They were resourceful. They were armed with unimaginable technology and almost infinite time. They could fix it." I pause. "Is this crazy enough yet?"

"Pretty crazy. Why sixty-three million years?"

"I'll get to that. But first . . . what does a homesteader do with new land? The very first thing?"

She shrugs. "Plant it?"

"No, before that he clears it. He removes the rocks and cuts the trees. He plows it. Then, if he can, he plants a cover crop to improve the soil. To make it more productive. Okay?"

She nods.

"So, first off, these . . . Farmers . . . they crash a massive asteroid into the planet. That kills off all the dinosaurs and opens up the land for a new species. For a new crop, if you will."

"And that was what happened sixty-three million years ago?"

"Yes. If what I'm suggesting is true. Should I go on? This gets even weirder."

"Please," she says, settling back into the cushions.

"Well, the asteroid creates volcanos and clouds of ash that block out the sunlight, but it doesn't really fix the atmosphere problem. They needed more carbon. More heat. So they planted a cover crop. Not plants, but animals. Animals genetically engineered to increase in number and evolve and cover the earth. To do the work for them. To eventually extract all the oil and the coal and the natural gas and all of the other fossil fuels buried in the planet's crust and burn them in the atmosphere to increase the carbon dioxide and other greenhouse gasses. The temperature would rise to suit the Farmers. Carbon dioxide would become adequately abundant. I don't know, maybe they photosynthesize. I have no idea what the Farmers are."

"And in the process," Suzanne speculates, "the cover crop would self-destruct. Would annihilate itself. By changing the climate and poisoning the atmosphere."

"Exactly. Like clearing a field with Roundup. Cleansing the path. So when the Farmers come back, the planet would be unoccupied. The climate would be adjusted to suit them. The ground would be ready for the cash crop. Those lovers of dry dunes and blowing sand and carbon-rich air would move in."

"Millions of years later," she muses. "The time scale is . . . is impossible to imagine."

"Yes," I say. "Living eternally must offer a different perspective of time."

"But what if the species . . . the cover crop . . . what if someone in the cover crop figures it all out? What if they decide to stop generating the lethal greenhouse gasses?"

"They can't," I respond.

"Why not?"

"Remember, they are genetically engineered for a single purpose. They are programmed to indulge only their own short term gain. They are programmed so they *cannot* do a single thing about it. That would go against their nature."

"That's crazy," she says.

"Yes."

"And the visions? What about them? The tower?"

I shake my head. "I don't know. Maybe messages home. I don't know."

"And the clouds?" she asks.

"I don't know."

"Communication structures? Monitoring stations maybe?"

"I don't know. Maybe the clouds are the Farmers themselves. I just don't know. Or maybe they have nothing at all to do with it."

She sits quietly. Silently I watch her, waiting for a verdict.

"What if this is all true?" she asks at last, her dark eyes troubled. "Now that you've figured it out, what do you plan to do?"

I shrug. "Nothing, I guess."

"But . . . but that would be horrible, wouldn't it? The whole idea kind of shoots the hell out of trying to plan your life."

Slowly I shake my head. "Not really. Not so horrible. Nothing has changed. It's not so different from what they teach at the abbey. The Zen

universe is a cold place. In our short lives, it won't make much difference. After we are dead, it will matter even less. Besides, there *is*
nothing we can do about it. Don't you see, it doesn't make one scintilla
of difference whether we were designed by an alien race of Farmers or by
a blind process of natural selection. They produce the same result: a
species incapable of giving up short-term gain for long term sanity.
Think about it."

"But . . . ."

"Let me read you something from that little book of yours," I say.
"The one beside your bed–"

"Ikkyū?"

"Yes. I'm sorry. I hope you don't mind that I was reading it . . ."

"Not at all," she says. "I love Ikkyū."

I pad into her room to fetch the book. "Things are no different now
than when Ikkyū wrote these verses," I say as I return. Thumbing through
the passages, I settle onto the sofa beside her. "I never read him before.
These verses seem so . . . for me anyway . . . they seem so . . . so
poignant. One passage in particular struck me." I find my place. "Let
me read it to you."

She nods.

I read, "*Delusion makes it appear that though the body dies, the
soul endures–this is a grave error. The enlightened declare that both
body and soul perish together. 'Buddha' is emptiness, and heaven and
earth return to the original ground of being.*"

"I know those lines," she says. "From 'Skeletons.' I've read them
a hundred times."

I glance up, then continue, "*I've set aside the eighty thousand books
of scripture and given you the essence in this slim volume.*" I close the
book and set it beside me. "In the end," I say, "after we are gone, what
does it matter *why* we have poisoned the planet?"

A shiver passes through her. "I'm cold," she says. "Will you hold
me?"

I slide over to her. Circle my arm gently around her slender
shoulders. Cradle her. Suzanne is trembling. I draw her closer. Rub her
neck. Stroke her hair. I comfort her. Both of us are wearing our priestly
robes. This irony would have pleased Ikkyū beyond measure.

She snuggles her head against my chest. It feels wonderful.

"You are ten years younger than I am," I whisper with a last vestige of propriety. "I'm too old for you."

She lifts her face. Her dark eyes are soft and moist. "Ikkyū had his Lady Mori," she whispers. "He was in his seventies while she was still a young woman."

"She was blind," I remind her.

"We are all blind," she replies. "They loved each other."

"Yes," I say. "They loved each other."

"And he wrote such beautiful verses about their lovemaking."

"That's what we remember, isn't it?" I whisper. "That's what lasts." I am still for a long time, holding her, rocking her. "Ikkyū and Lady Mori. We remember them even though they have been dead for a long, long time."

"Ah," Suzanne smiles, snuggling closer and slipping her small hand onto my chest beneath my robe, "but while they were alive . . . ."

Balance

The sun had ducked beneath the shelf of high overcast and entered the seam that separated earth and sky, firing horizontal rays through the upstairs window where Jericho Ban sat gazing out. In slow motion the fiery ball melted over the hills at the edge of the world. He watched as the slanting beams rose to light the bottoms of the gray clouds, revealing creams and pinks that the vaporous monsters had been concealing all day long. Across the storybook town smoke had begun to rise and curl from storybook chimneys above storybook roofs that fit together like scattered pieces of an indecipherable jigsaw puzzle.

All day thunderstorms had rumbled through, wetting the grass, bouncing hail stones off the roof and pavement and then opening their arms to allow the sky to inspect their work. With the sun gone, the cold, which had been there all along, hiding in dark corners or else riding the sharp edge of the breeze, began to reassert its dominion.

"The silvery winter of dispersed radiation," Jericho said to himself as he gazed out over the rooftops at the gathering gloom. *That's what Loren Eiseley had called it.* He settled more comfortably into his chair and his ruminations, letting his eyelids droop. *We are all sunlight, aren't we? Squeezed together. Water. Carbon dioxide. Pinches of trace materials. Twisted and spun into amino acids. Woven and rewoven into DNA. Incubated within cell walls. Bound together in sinews. Bone. Hanks of hair. Crowned by a blob of gray mass folded back upon itself to sustain the electrochemical dance of thought. We are all sunlight. Sunlight captured for a while as human, later to be dissolved, disintegrated, and released back again into the void as a whimper of entropy.*

"Jeri?"

"Mmm," he managed, opening his eyes and swivelling in his chair. Phoebe stood framed in the darkened doorway, illuminated by the fading light outside the window. His lovely Phoebe. Her head was turned away as if she were listening for something deep inside the house behind her.

Her blond pony tail splayed out from the back of her head like a golden bouquet. He had not heard her climb the stairs. Perhaps he had dozed. From memory he heard what she might have asked: *"You didn't hear a word I was saying, did you?"* Her voice trailed off, fading with the light.

He averted his eyes. He couldn't help himself. He didn't want to see the other side of her head when she turned to face him. The street light on the corner outside winked on and washed the room with its yellow sodium glare. And when he glanced back, she was gone. Of course she was gone.

"Phoebe," he mouthed the word, but only to himself, and shivered. *Chilled to the bone, they used to say.* Jericho leaned forward and stiffly pried himself up into an awkward hunch. *Chilled to the soul is more like it.*

Not fully awake, he retreated down the stairs, trying not to think about what lay ahead at the meeting that night. He went through the motions of heating a frozen chicken pot pie in the microwave and washing and shredding a head of lettuce. He ate supper in silence without much appetite. Doc Proffer had told him it would come back with time, but it hadn't. Not yet. Mechanically he washed and stacked the dishes in the drainer. He was tired. He hadn't slept well lately. It left him in a strange state of disassociation. His mind was elsewhere. His body ran on instinct. To keep alert, he was drinking too much coffee.

Jericho climbed back up the stairs to the bedroom to pull on a clean shirt, trousers, and a navy blue wool sweater for the meeting. Still he avoided thinking about the agenda. He would preside as mayor at the city council meeting that evening, as he had presided at meeting after meeting for too long. He was tired of it all, but Doc Proffer had said that civic involvement would be good for him. It would help to lift his spirits. But it hadn't. Not really.

At the big captain's desk in the front parlor he settled into the creaking office chair and switched on the goose-neck lamp. It had been her father's desk. Her father's chair. Her father's house. Phoebe's father. His father-in-law. Now it was his. All this. His legacy from the old man's hand-written will. Now all this was his.

Now, he sighed. *Now it is time to think about the council meeting.* From his worn leather briefcase he pulled out the thick packet that had been delivered to his front door last Friday by a reserve deputy from the city police department. He had already glanced through the agenda and supporting materials before hiding them away from the light of day in his old friend the briefcase. But now it was time to reckon with them.

Unbelievable, he confirmed as he reread the first two items of business. The only business of any gravity. Two urgency ordinances, each claiming to be necessary for the immediate preservation of the public peace, health, and safety. The ordinance receiving a majority vote of the five council members would go into effect immediately. The facts constituting the necessity were recited in each ordinance. They were the same facts, worded differently. Jericho had read them when they first arrived. Now he couldn't bring himself to read those words again. Neither ordinance should have been there, but that both were there together was preposterous.

From the edge of the desk he removed his gavel and sound block and placed them in the bottom of the briefcase. Without much consideration, he lifted the heavy velvet drawstring sack from the left-hand bottom desk drawer and laid it in beside the gavel and block. He covered them with the thickened city council folder and a pad of yellow paper. It was time to go.

As he pulled the front door shut, Jericho remembered that he needed to make another appointment with the psychologist. *Another psychologist.* The "grief counselor," Doc Proffer had called him when he made the referral. Jericho had phoned for an appointment, but he hadn't kept it. He hadn't felt like washing his dirty laundry in public. Anyway, he figured he could tough it out until things got better. He could find his own balance. Only he hadn't found balance. And now that his sleep was haunted by vivid repetitions of the old horror, night after night, he was no longer so sure. A vital essence was draining out of him.

The meeting had been moved from the council chambers to Prasch Hall because an overflow crowd was anticipated. The cavernous auditorium usually served as a skating rink and basketball court, and the echoing acoustics were atrocious. On the street outside the building two network tv vans had pointed their communications dishes toward the heavens. This sort of thing did not happen in Blue Lake.

"Excuse me," someone in a rain slicker called at him through the cold drizzle as he passed beneath the last streetlight. "Mayor Ban. Can I have a word with you?"

Jericho picked up his pace and diagonaled for the double doors at the front of the barn-like building.

"Mayor Ban," the reporter persisted, pursuing him with a microphone held like a baton he had just received from the camera man on his heels. "Do you intend to recuse yourself from the vote tonight?"

"Now why would I do that?" he smiled without slowing.

"Well . . . you know . . . your wife–"

Jericho made it through the front door. A young city police officer in a blue uniform was stationed there. "Mayor," he nodded respectfully. Behind him at the skate rental counter the Chief of Police was engaged with two sheriff's deputies in their distinctive tan outfits. *Thank God for mutual aid*, Jericho thought.

Bright blue-tinged mercury vapor lights buzzed in aluminum saucers that glared down from the ceiling. He felt like he had stepped into an x-ray machine. It was a carnival inside. Already the hall was almost full. Fifty folding chairs were occupied and an overflow crowd milled restlessly behind them and on the sidelines. Most of the faces were not local. Many of the out-of-towners displayed signs and banners which Jericho made an effort not to read. He was in a foreign country. At the focal point of the audience stood three long folding trestle tables, erected as a ground-level podium, and the public works crew was setting up microphones for each council member and the city manager and one at the lectern for public input. The sound was all being fed through the permanent public address system that usually blared thumping motivational music for the skaters. At a control panel on a card table a young man Jericho didn't recognize was attempting to squelch the piercing screech of feedback.

Josh Ostertag, the new City Manager, scurried over to him as Jericho was setting down his heavy briefcase on the floor at the center of the folding tables. Two local reporters had been following the manager, but Ostertag waved them away. "I tried to call you all weekend," he said.

Jericho could barely hear him above the reverberations of crowd. "I unplugged my phone," he shouted.

"And I came over to your house twice."

"Wasn't answering the door."

The City Manager nodded. Accepted the information. Digested it. He was a slender young man, swarthy with hair already beginning to thin on top. The council had just hired him on a split vote. He had good educational credentials, but little experience. Ostertag nodded again. "How do you plan to handle this?" he yelled.

"I'm going to call both items up at the same time. If the council doesn't object. Let the public address either one as they please. It's all the same thing anyway."

"That could shorten it a bit, I guess. You plan to limit each speaker to three minutes?"

"That's what I was hoping. That's what the council agreed last time. Did you bring the timer?"

The City Manager reached into his jacket pocket and extracted a little square plastic device and showed him which button to push to start and which to reset. Liquid crystal numbers flashed on and began to count down. "I already set it for three minutes."

"I see you've got the police on standby," Jericho said. "Who's in charge?"

"Chief'll be calling the shots," Ostertag said. "Sheriff loaned us two deputies."

"Have we got anything from the City Attorney? She gonna be here?"

"Nope. She's in Italy. Vacation with her daughter. But she sent an email you can read." He handed Jericho a single sheet of paper with a short paragraph at the top.

Jericho glanced at it. The attorney apologized for missing the meeting and noted that she had serious reservations that either of the ordinances would pass constitutional muster. "Jesus!" he exclaimed. "This is it?"

"That's it. You're on your own. You want to continue the hearing until she can be here?"

Jericho glanced around the boisterous crowd just as the electronic alarm sounded in the palm of his hand. He punched the off button. "Too late for that. Maybe after the hearing. You'll do a lead in?"

"I can read the titles of each of the ordinances and explain their effects," the City Manager offered. "But then you're on your own. I didn't have anything to do with drafting them, you know."

"I know," Jericho nodded and set the little timer on the table.

"And this's above my pay grade anyway," Ostertag grumbled as he walked away.

Jericho looked around to see how many of the council members had showed up. He had not spoken to any of them. Clarence "Buck" Diggins stood off to one side, near a group wearing NRA buttons, gesticulating briskly to two men in expensive suits. Buck was a stringy old fellow with the wattled neck of a turkey vulture and eyes that burned with a fierce intensity, if not intelligence. His skin bore an unhealthy gray pallor and hung off his bones in folds that could have been inhabited by a man twice his size. Pale white wisps of gossamer ringed his pate, mottled with liver spots, and tufts of the same stuff bristled from his nose and ears. Buck had served on the city council from time immemorial and in his aw-shucks Oklahoma twang never tired of reminding them all of what the town had been like in the good old days when the mill was still running. Alive and humming, it had been. When the diesel logging trucks started growling hours before sunrise. When the smoky haze from the teepee burners reddened and flavored the air. Those were the sounds and the smells of progress. Progress and jobs.

Buck had been mayor when Jericho was elected to fill a council vacancy nearly four years ago. He had continued to serve as mayor for two more years until the next election, when his supporters couldn't find three votes to reelect him or agree on anyone else. One newly elected member and the two old members who had grown weary of Buck's aimless ranting and inept shepherding of meetings, which often droned on well after midnight, selected Jericho on a split vote to take over the reins as mayor. That vote had enraged Buck and embittered him against Jericho and his "commie" leanings.

It was Buck who had brought all this fuss to a head by introducing the second of the two urgency ordinances they would be considering tonight. He had managed to get it on the agenda first. Buck wasn't smart enough to have drafted it himself, so Jericho suspected the two men who were indulging him on the edge of the crowd.

He looked around for the others. Vivian Beecher caught his eye and waved. She wore a happy blue and white flowery blouse. Vivian was the newest council member, a housewife with three small children at home. She often didn't have a clue what was going on. But she was polite and friendly and seemed to admire Jericho. She followed his lead in the discussions and voted as he did. He smiled at her and waved back.

Veronica Tucker dropped her bag on the seat next to him on his left. "'Evening, Jericho," she said cheerily. "Looks like we got quite a night ahead of us. Did ya bring your toothbrush and pillow?"

"No," he laughed. "I think I can get us through this sooner than you might think." He studied her as she unpacked her bag onto the table. He liked her well enough, even though she usually sided with old Buck in the discussions and voting. But that was to be expected. Like Buck, Veronica had grown up in Blue Lake. Her father had been a logger here. Her husband drove a log truck until the work was cut back. Now they subsisted on his unemployment benefits and her wages as a part-time waitress, waiting for social security to kick in. Like Buck, she could remember as a child the belching teepee burners, the roar of the log and lumber trucks, and the raucous, hard-drinking logger bars downtown.

Jericho searched for Carleson's rotund shape. He didn't see the fifth council member anywhere. *Where is Carleson?* He sat down and began spreading out his things. The yellow pad he placed just there by his right hand. His pens beside it. The file to his left. Like a chess master deploying his pieces, he moved the microphone to the left a little bit, then brought it back to make room for the timer. When everything was right, he searched the faces of the crowd again. *Where the hell is Carleson? Without Carleson everything would be out of balance. Unbalanced.* He smiled to himself. *Everything is unbalanced already.* He leaned over, snapped his briefcase shut, and waited while one after another Veronica, Buck, and Vivian took their seats. He looked at his watch. It was already seven o'clock, but still no Carleson. "Let's give him a few more minutes," he said, though no one could hear him above the racket.

At five after seven, Jericho leaned into his microphone. "Well, I guess we should get started." The sound reverberated off the bare walls in a disorienting manner. "Has anyone heard from Mr. Carleson?"

There was a commotion at the front door and Edgar Carleson, in his rusty corduroy blazer with leather elbow patches and a white silk tie, strode through at the head of a retinue of a dozen college students wearing backpacks and fresh young faces. *He was waiting to make his grand entrance*, Jericho thought with annoyance. Carleson, with his flowing auburn hair and neatly trimmed, red-tinged beard, was a popular professor in the Natural Resources Department at the university in Arcata, a spokesman for a number of environmental committees, causes, and cliques, and above all else, a showman who would have been better suited for the Theater Arts Department. A chorus of cheers was met with boos as he wound his way through the center of the auditorium to settle his bulk theatrically into his chair at the opposite end of the tables from old Buck. The three tables had been hinged forward at the outside to form an arc that allowed the two adversaries to glare directly across at each other.

"Sorry I'm late," Carleson lilted into his microphone with a sonorous baritone, "but I had some important preparations to complete."

"Now that we're all present," Jericho continued, ignoring the apology, "I'm going to call this meeting of the Blue Lake City Council to order." He tapped the gavel a single time. "Because we are getting a late start and we have a lot of people in the audience who want to be heard, I propose dispensing with the flag salute and postponing the reading of the minutes, the committee reports, and the general public comments to the end of the meeting. Are there any objections from the council?"

No one offered any objection.

"Alright then. Hearing no objection, we'll move on to the agenda. Again . . . this is a little irregular . . . but I think we can move along faster and get more complete public input if I call both items 4 and 5 at the same time. They're the two urgency ordinances and both arise from the same urgency. In that way, the public can address either or both and we will actually have only one public hearing instead of–"

"I think we ought a'call item 4 first all by itself," Buck broke in. "That's *my* ord'nance an' it shouldn't take all that long and we won't even have t'get to the other one if–"

"He's out of order," raged Carleson. "The Mayor hasn't recognized Buck–"

The crowd scented blood and issued a cacophony of hoots and cat calls.

Jericho tapped his gavel and raised both arms. "Gentlemen! Gentlemen, *please*!" The hall slowly quieted. "Now I'm going to make a procedural motion here that will take precedence over everything else. I move we call items 4 and 5 tegether at the same time to expedite the hearings. Is there a second?"

Vivian to his right obediently seconded the motion.

"Now . . . as a procedural motion, there will be no further discussion. All in favor signify by saying 'aye.'"

Tucker and Beecher both voted "aye." Carleson thought about it before adding his "aye."

"Aye," said Jericho. "All opposed, signify by saying 'nay.'"

"Nay," stormed Buck. "This just ain't right—"

Jericho tapped the gavel. "The ayes have it. The motion carries. I will now call both items 4 and 5 from the agenda. We'll have a brief introduction of the two ordinances by the City Manager, then open the public hearing to take input from the audience. Council discussion will follow the closing of the public hearing. Mr. City Manager."

Ostertag sucked in a quick breath, then read the first title. "'Ordinance No. 947, an Urgency Ordinance of the City of Blue Lake Requiring Every Resident of the City to Possess and Maintain in His Residence at All Times a Loaded and Fully Operable Firearm.' This ordinance would require—"

Suddenly Buck broke in, cutting him off. He lips were inches from his microphone and his voice boomed through the auditorium, "That's my ord'nance, an' I think it's all pretty clear an' we don't need a whole lotta jawbonin' 'bout it—"

"He's out of order," Carleson screamed into his mike. "Mr. Mayor, Diggins is out of order—"

"I'll show you whose's outta order," Buck hollered, shaking a balled fist at Carleson.

Jericho grabbed the gavel and banged it on the sound block. "That's enough. Both of you—"

Buck was on his feet now, bending over his microphone like an ungainly stork. "I fought fer you-all's freedom in two wars," he screeched.

"Mr. Mayor—"

"Two wars!" Buck shouted.

"Mr. Mayor–"

Jericho pounded the gavel hard enough to split the block.

But Buck was just reaching his stride. He had himself an audience and wasn't about to let go. "An' I ain't a'gonna let no red commie . . . pinko . . . draft-dodgin' . . . whippersnappers . . . deprive me o' my freedom o' speech . . . or hammer me down–"

The audience loved it. This was better than the live extreme kick-boxing they were missing on tv. This was exactly what many had come to see. Jericho caught the eye of the sound board man and drew his fingers across his throat.

A scraggly young man had leapt to the lectern and was just beginning to shout "Let ol' Buck talk–" when the microphones went dead. A cheer went up from one side, but was hooted down from across the auditorium. Police and sheriffs deputies inserted themselves between the council and the crowd, wading into it to order the most vocal to pipe down or be arrested. Slowly the noise level dropped and a semblance of order returned.

Jericho drew a deep breath and gave a thumbs-up to the sound man, then spoke calmly into his microphone. "Is this on? Okay. Thank you. It's going to be a long night, folks, so I want to do this in as orderly a manner as possible. Please be patient. Everyone is going to have a chance to be heard. But one at a time. Now, because Councilman Diggins has already begun to make a motion, I'm going to let him finish what he started. Briefly, I hope. Then we're going to finish hearing what the City Manager has to say on *both* ordinances before we open it up for public comment. After that, the council will have its turn. Is that alright with the council?"

Carleson started to say something, then thought better of it. One by one, the members all acquiesced.

"Buck? You can finish your piece, but please be brief. You'll get a chance to add as much as you want after the public hearing."

Buck leaned over his microphone. "I just want'a say . . . I want'a say that this's *my* ordinance, an' it's pretty dang simple. It's jus' like the one they passed in a town no bigger'n this in Georgia, an' that one's stood up. So yer either with me on this here, or yer again' me. I'm a'callin' for a vote on 'er. Right now. Up'er down. Let's vote on it an' git on home."

Hoots of agreement and protest rose from the audience.

Jericho pounded his gavel. "What's the pleasure of the council?" he asked. "Is there a second to Buck's motion calling for the question right now?"

"I don't think we can do that without the public hearing first," Carlson observed. "Brown Act requires public input."

The City Manager straightened like a turtle pulling its head out of its shell. "I think that's right, Mr. Mayor," he said. "You'll have to do the public hearing first."

Council members looked at each other and seemed to agree. No one offered a second to Buck's motion.

"All right then." Jericho tapped the gavel. "Motion dies for lack of a second. Let's proceed. Mr. Ostertag?"

"Thank you, Mr. Mayor. I'll now read the title of Ordinance 948. 'Ordinance No. 948, an Urgency Ordinance of the City of Blue Lake Prohibiting the Possession, Discharge, or Activation of Any Weapon System, Firearm, or Explosive Within the City Limits, Including, but Not Limited to, Handguns, Rifles, Shotguns, and Ammunition.'"

The hooting and cat-calling began even before he had finished. Pro-NRA placards began bouncing and waving dangerously. Jericho pounded it all down with the gavel. The sheriff's deputies clamped onto the arms of one particularly belligerent character and escorted him to the front door.

When the hall had quieted enough to hear, Ostertag said, "The titles pretty much speak for themselves. One ordinance requires everyone to have a gun. The other prohibits everyone from having one. These are both urgency ordinances and go into effect immediately on adoption." That was it.

Things were moving swiftly. Jericho tapped the gavel and announced, "I'm now going to open the public hearing. Our council rules limit each speaker to three minutes, so you'll want to get right to the point."

Someone shouted, "What if I got more than three minute's worth t'say?"

"Then go back to the end of the line. I'll hold up my hand when your time is up."

Behind the lectern a line had formed, which wound around behind the chairs and became indistinct in the verges of the crowd. The first speaker was a heavy-set young man with closely-cropped hair wearing a camouflage jumpsuit that bore an NRA button. He advanced on the lectern with purpose and gripped it firmly with both hands. "Mr. Mayor," his voice boomed, "do you intend to step down from this decision?"

The auditorium grew quiet.

"I mean," the speaker went on, "are you going to disqualify yourself?"

After a long pause, Jericho leaned into his microphone. "Your time is running out. Do you have anything more to add, sir? This is not a question and answer session. This is your opportunity to make comments to the entire city council. Do you have anything else you want to say?"

This flustered the speaker, and he did not like being flustered in front of an auditorium brimming with onlookers and tension. "Well *I* for one damn' well think you *ought* to step down. We all know about you. You ain't no impartial judge, not by a long shot, an' we all know it. If this was a trial in court, a judge'd never let you sit on the jury. No way. Not with what happened to your wife."

"Nay, sir, I have no wife," Jericho heard himself say. "Why do you speak of such a thing?" *Where was this gibberish coming from? Wasn't that a line from Hamlet?*

"You're wife was shot dead at the Sunburst Charter School massacre in Arcata, wasn't she?"

"She shore as shootin' was," Buck broke in. "Shot half her head right off–"

"*Enough!*" Jericho shouted at the councilman. "You'll get your turn." He glared back at the man gripping the lectern. "Do you have a wife, sir?" he heard himself ask.

The man ignored him and began reading a newspaper account of the bloody shooting two years earlier, while the council members all turned to study their Mayor. "It says right here . . . let's see . . . elementary school shooting . . . seventeen first graders gunned down . . . visiting school psychologist Phoebe Ban was hit by a bullet in the right temple

. . . "

Jericho was suddenly angry. He watched his hand bang the gavel until the man stopped speaking. "I asked you, sir, do you have a wife?"

"Well, yeah . . . she's right char." A mousy woman in a matching camo outfit raised her hand tentatively.

Jericho continued, "And if I were to slaughter your wife in cold blood like an innocent lamb, do you think that should deprive you of your right to speak here today?"

"Well . . . no . . . but–"

"Then your time's up. Next speaker."

"Let 'im talk," someone shouted. Several others hollered their agreement, but the camo man had vacated the lectern with his head hung down. Something in his posture made Jericho sorry for the way he had handled him. Something had broken loose inside. He had lost his balance. He determined to get it back. And keep his mouth shut, uncertain what might come out if he opened it again.

The speakers began their long and seemingly endless precession to the lectern. Most abandoned the podium when Jericho raised his hand, but for several he had to have the microphone cut. One firebrand held his position, waiving a sign that read "Second Amendment, Issued 12/15/1791, Expires: Never" until he too was escorted out by the deputies. Another with a placard reading "I'd rather have a gun in my hand than a cop on the phone" sat down and refused to budge until the deputies dragged him out through the dangerous cat-calling crowd. A little while later two more deputies and a Highway Patrol officer arrived as backup. The gun-control advocates, though clearly outnumbered, were no less confrontational and strident. The comments grew repetitive, but even if it added nothing, each speaker demanded his or her three minutes in the political limelight.

Jericho would have liked to have heard what the two men in the fine suits had to say, but they never spoke. They lurked in the background like cancerous genes turning on the malignancies expressed by others. As the public hearing droned on, Jericho passed the time by studying the signs and placards. Behind Buck they boasted themes like "NRA, We Do Our Part" and "Gun Control–Use Both Hands" and "Not Gun Control, Just Control." On the other side of the hall the signs read "Guns Kill" and "How Much Is A Life Worth?" and "Amend The Second Amendment" and "NRA Not Relevant Anymore" and "Gun Control Now!"

The arguments grew turbulent and draining as the mercury lights buzzed down like a desert sun that seemed to suck the air out of the room. After a while Jericho could scarcely distinguish between the rants of the two sides. The strutting and the posturing and the venom and the finger-pointing caused a sour anger to rise deep inside. The lofty oratory about the devastation caused by guns in the wrong hands made the anger churn and spread like an infection through his blood. They had no idea. *They had no fucking idea!*

At some point a crimson curtain seemed to draw itself across his mind and Jericho stopped listening. But the membrane was semi-permeable, and through it diffused the same words and phrases over and over again. "Sandy Hook Elementary School." "Virginia Tech." "Aurora, Colorado." "Tucson." "Columbine." And the words pronounced more than any others: "Arcata" and "Sunburst School Shooting." Then all eyes would turn and fix on him, Jericho Ban, as if it were all his fault. As if passing judgment. Then he would flinch and close his eyes. *Guilty as charged.*

And then, just as he felt he could stand it no longer, it was all over. The lectern stood empty. Jericho looked for stragglers. Seeing none, he banged the gavel. "I declare this public hearing closed. Let's all take a short break. Ten minutes."

The lines for the bathrooms were long, but the council members were allowed to move to the front. By this time of night, the crowd should have abated, but most people stayed on. The outcome still hung in the balance. And like fans at a sporting event, they all wanted to see if their team would win.

Fifteen minutes later Jericho struck the gavel again. "Council discussion," he said.

Carleson was the first to wade in. "Sandy Hook school. Twenty first-graders killed. *First graders!* Six staffers killed. Aurora Theater. Twelve dead. Seventy injured. Starburst Montessori School. Right in our own backyard. Seven preschoolers killed. Three staff members killed, including the wife of our own mayor. Phoebe Ban. Many of you knew her. She was a beautiful young woman. Involved in the community. Senselessly struck down in the prime of her life . . ."

A surge of anger flashed in Jericho's breast. Suddenly he despised Carleson and all the others who wanted to use Phoebe for their own political advantage. It felt as if Carleson's filthy tongue had sullied the memory of something he had no right to touch.

". . . I ask you this," Carleson went on, "*How much is enough?*" That got the crowd wound up, and he kept them at a fevered pitch as he ridiculed Buck and his mandatory gun-ownership ordinance. "I know, I know, it doesn't apply to a 'conscientious objector.' I assume that means anyone who doesn't want a gun in his or her home. But by including that exemption, the stupid ordinance doesn't do anything at all. *So why pass it?*"

"Because it makes a statement!" Buck broke in. "It makes a statement! Tells the world how we feel about draft dodgers and commies like you an'–"

Carleson waived him off in theatrical disgust. "I think I made my point. Let's adopt the common sense gun control ordinance and leave that other obscenity for the carrion eaters."

Jericho nodded. "Buck?"

Buck spoke of "his" ordinance again and reiterated what he had said at the beginning. But he didn't have anything new to add. It seemed clear that he hadn't read more than the title of either ordinance. But he ended strong with a few phrases he read from a sheet of paper. "'Those who are bent on committing evil will continue to commit evil regardless of legislation and additional laws. The gun control ord'nance' – that's the *other* 'un – 'will penalize law-abiding citizens and won't do anything to curb gun violence.'" He looked up. "Not a lick o' good. An' the Fourth Amendment guarantees the right o' all o' us t'have our guns–"

"That's the *Second* Amendment, Buck," Carleson chided derisively. "The *Second* Amendment guarantees–"

"Yeah, *right*," Buck rejoined. "You *shut up* now, Mr. Smarty Pants. You already had yer say. An' the *Second* Amendment guarantees us all the right t'have our guns in our own houses. For our protection. Period." He thought for a moment, then added, "Why, if Phoebe Ban had been a'packin' a side arm two years ago, who knows how that whole thing might a turned out–"

"*Keep her out of this,*" Jericho growled.

But Buck hadn't heard him. "Poor Phoebe," he droned on. "We all knew her and liked her . . . an' if'n she had'a been packin'–"

Jericho pounded the gavel. "*That's enough of that!* Move on to something else."

Buck started to protest, but when he saw Jericho's eyes, he thought better of it. "Well that's it. Now, by passin' my ord'nance, I say we send a message out t' those who wanna take away our rights. Who wanna control us." He paused for effect. "*Over my dead body!*"

The hall exploded in hails and cheers and hoots and howls.

When it quieted, it was Veronica Tucker's turn. She was brief. "I own a gun," she said. "Always have. Always will. An' I know how to use it. Strictly for protection. My dad owned guns, an' so did my gran'dad. They taught me. It's a part of the old way of life here in Blue Lake. It's the way it's always been. An' as long as the ordinance says . . . Buck's ordinance says . . . that ya don't *haf t'have* a gun if it's against your conscience . . . an' that nut cases and felons still *can't* have 'em either . . . an' that's what it does say . . . well, then I think we ought a' pass it." The crowd erupted in support and opposition. "I'm votin' for it!" she hollered over the clamor.

That left Vivian Beecher and Jericho. She obviously wished that he would go first, but he nodded to her and said, "Vivian? Your turn."

She cleared her throat uncomfortably. "I don't like guns," she said, her voice barely audible. "I don't have much to add to what's already been said. And I guess I'll be voting against Buck's ordinance and for the gun control ordinance."

The boos and hisses seemed to outweigh the cheers and applause. But the auditorium quieted quickly as they all turned to Jericho for the deciding vote. The public hearing was finished. The other council members had each had their say. Now it was his turn. The deciding vote.

Jericho studied the agenda in his hands. The lights were too bright. Their humming seemed to set up a reverberation in his head, like the feedback from someone's microphone that wouldn't stop screeching. The buzzing seemed to contain and obscure something Phoebe was trying to whisper to him. He felt a little sick to his stomach.

He bent over, unsnapped the clasp on his briefcase, lifted out the heavy velvet drawstring bag, and laid it on the table with a thunk. As he straightened up, a wave of light-headedness passed over him. Carefully he untied the drawstring, pulled open the mouth of the bag, and withdrew his father-in-law's Smith & Wesson .38 Special snubnose revolver – the one the old man had used to fire a single bullet into his own brain in the upstairs bedroom of the old house down the street two months after the remains of his only daughter had been laid to rest. Jericho held it out in both hands like a spiritual offering for all the audience to see.

"This is what we are talking about," he recited slowly, turning from side to side for all to see. "This." A surreal hush had settled over the assembly, as in a dream. "This . . . this is what we are talking about."

The law enforcement officers were uneasy and exchanged glances, but the Chief shook his head. Jericho was not brandishing the firearm. He was showing the audience an important piece of evidence as an attorney might to a jury. The Chief smiled. It was a fine piece of theater.

The revolver's smooth steel held a sheen of oil beneath his fingers. Jericho had never fired it, nor any handgun for that matter, but after the coroner had returned it to him as its rightful heir under the old man's hand-drawn will, he had read up on this particular model on the Internet, and he had cleaned it and oiled it and practiced with the cylinder empty. And he had loaded this legacy with cartridges he had purchased on the web. Cartridges with 200 grains of smokeless powder and jacketed hollow-point bullets. No one else knew that, of course. He held the revolver over his head for all to admire. It's steel gleamed blue in the unblinking white mercury light. "This is what we are talking about," he repeated. "This."

Gripping the revolver with his right hand, careful to keep his fingers outside the trigger guard, he spread his left arm toward Buck. "Now Councilman Diggins here says . . . '*Protection.*' He says this firearm has a valid, even a holy use in protecting the safety of our children and our spouses and our community and ourselves." Jericho switched the gun to his other hand and raised his right arm toward Carleson. "Councilman Carlson says . . . '*Injury.*' He claims this thing brings only injury and death and devastation into our community." He returned the revolver to the table, setting it gently on top of the velvet sack, then raised both hands before him, palms upward like a balance scale, raising one while lowering the other. "All of the speakers we have listened to here so patiently have taken one position," he reversed the balance of his hands, "or the other." He lowered both hands to settle on the revolver. "So it seems clear that it is *not* the weapon itself that determines whether it is for protection or for injury . . . whether it is good or evil . . . but it is the intention of the person wielding it." He looked from face to face of the audience he held spellbound, while they waited to see which way his discourse would break. "But what if *both* extremes are equally at fault? Think about it. What if the fault itself lies in the dehumanizing and vilifying of those who do not agree with you?"

Jericho drew a deep breath, grasping at last what Phoebe expected from him. He set his jaw. He was no longer angry, just in pain. "Let me demonstrate."

He regripped the revolver in both hands, flipping off the safety and drawing back the hammer with his thumb, and swung it swiftly to point at the center of the chest of Councilman Clarence "Buck" Diggins. The pistol lurched violently in Jericho's hands with a terrifying explosion that sent shockwaves through the auditorium and reverberated in the public address speakers. The power of the bullet knocked frail Buck over backwards in his chair, his feet flying up over his head.

With his ears ringing and tears beginning to stream down his face, Jericho swung the revolver in a smooth arc to his right as he pulled back the hammer and aimed it at Carleson's presumptuous white necktie, where it draped across his breastbone. Carleson was grinning like a predatory cat, as if he had just seen his dear comrade rip open a cage and eat the evil canary inside. He had no inkling that the canary was at the bottom of the mine shaft. He half rose, not in fear, but in a twisted sort of congratulations, when the second hollow-point exploded across the council table and blew him back into his chair. A red rose blossomed out of the hole in the silky fabric of his tie.

The auditorium erupted with cries and shouts of horror. Everyone stampeded for the exit doors, or else dove for cover behind the flimsy stand of folding chairs. The police and sheriff's deputies had drawn their weapons and were trying to crouch into stable firing positions, but were buffeted by the screaming crowd. Jericho dropped the smoking revolver onto the fiberglass table with a clunk that was picked up by the sound system and amplified through the chaotic hall as a final punctuation. Jericho blotted his eyes with his sleeve and leaned into the microphone to make his voice heard above the roar of terror.

"*Now*," his voice thundered. "What have we proved? *Nothing!* We have proved nothing." He paused to let the clarity of his reasoning sink in. "And since there will be no further discussion from the City Council, I will now call for the question. All in favor of adopting ordinance 947 – that's the one requiring everyone to possess a firearm – all in favor say 'aye.'"

On either side of him Council members Tucker and Beecher sat frozen in their seats like deer caught in a spotlight. Neither even whimpered.

"All opposed," Jericho continued, "signify by saying 'nay' . . . *nay*. The motion fails on a vote of zero to one. Now . . . all in favor of adopting ordinance 948 – that's the one prohibiting possession of all firearms – say 'aye.'" Again no one spoke. "All opposed, say 'nay' . . . *nay*. The nays have it. The motion fails by the same vote. Now . . . turning to the next item of business on the agenda–"

But he never got to the next item of business. His own Chief of Police grabbed him around the neck and threw him to the polished hardwood skating floor, cuffing his wrists behind him, while the other officers stood over them with guns drawn. He was half-dragged and half-pushed through the pandemonium to a waiting police car outside while the tv cameras rolled. Roughly they handled him, but Jericho didn't mind. He understood. They were justifiably angry. He had led them down a path and then betrayed them.

Jericho Ban was only a single person, an insignificant one at that, who had suffered an insufferable wrong. But for a moment, if only a moment, he had managed to restore a modicum of balance to a wildly wobbling world. He couldn't remember ever feeling more at peace with himself.

Revelation

More than two decades ago, on my fiftieth birthday, I backpacked alone to Papoose Lake high in the Trinity Alps Wilderness. Climbing to a gap in the head wall overlooking the lake, I sat on a smooth white boulder and surveyed the dazzling glacier-polished granite slab stretching far and away into the distance. The sun was hot. A breeze tousled my hair. I was almost dozing, when God appeared.

"Before now," He said, "I have never appeared unto any man."

"Whoa," I said, flattered and dumbfounded.

"And I've never told anyone what to do."

"Never?" I said. "Hold on . . . what about Moses . . . the ten commandments?"

"Not My message," God replied.

"What about Jesus . . . and Mohammed . . . and Joseph Smith . . . and all the others who've written down Your messages?"

"Not Mine."

"Messages from your messengers?"

"Nope."

"Your angels, then, acting on their own?"

"No. It doesn't work that way."

"Huh." I scratched my head. "Then where did those messages come from? Satan? Were they delusions? Or manipulative tools of control freaks?"

"Never mind that," God said dismissively. "That's not what I want to talk about."

"Okay. What then?"

"Can you do something for Me?"

"Er . . . I don't know," I answered cautiously. "What did You have in mind?"

"I'd like you to carry a message back to all mankind. Spread the word."

"Well, that's not really my thing. I've got kind of a busy schedule
. . . ."

"No rush. Fit it in when you have the time."

I pondered uncomfortably for a moment. "Are you sure You've got
the right messenger here?"

"Don't worry about that."

"Uh . . . so what's the message?"

"Just this: *Until now, I have never appeared unto any man, and I
have never told anyone what to do.*"

"Ah . . . like you were saying."

"Yes."

"Seems simple enough."

"Can you repeat it back?"

"Don't know why not," I said. "'Until now . . . You have never
appeared unto any man . . . and . . . er . . . You've never told anybody
what to do . . .'"

"Close enough. You'll do it, then?"

"What's the . . . ah . . . time frame on this?" I asked, postponing
commitment.

"Your choice. Okay? No time limit."

"Well . . . just how am I supposed to spread this message?"

"Again, your choice. You'll do it?"

I sighed. "I guess so. No one's going to believe me, though. I
suppose You know that."

"I know everything."

"Why bother then?"

"That's not what I came to reveal to you." He began to *fade*. "Do
it on faith."

"Wait a second," I said, standing, dizzy in the blinding sunlight. "Is
that it?"

"That's it." His empty voice whisked across the sepulchral white
stone. I could see the ragged spires of Sawtooth Peak manifesting
through His dissolving form.

I shouted, "Will I be seeing You again?"

With the timbre of wind rustling through tall grass, I believe I heard
Him say, "No one will be seeing Me again." And He was gone.

So that's it. That's my message. Or rather God's message. Take it or leave it. I've done my job.

About the Author

Richard S. Platz maintained a solo law practice in Humboldt County, California, for 35 years. He served as City Attorney for the City of Blue Lake for 32 of those years before retiring there in 2009. In addition to short stories, the author has written other novels, including *Appointment At Angahuan* (with James A. Kline), *Of Magic and Delusion*, and *Project Divine Wind*. He has also written short stories, poetry, and articles on various topics, including *Backpacking in Jefferson*, which can be read on his website: www.richardplatz.com.